NEW YORK REVIEW BOOKS
CLASSICS

COMMAND PERFORMANCE

JEAN ECHENOZ was born in 1947 in Vaucluse, France. He is the author of more than a dozen novels, including *Cherokee*, *Double Jeopardy*, *Chopin's Move*, *Big Blondes*, *Piano*, *Ravel*, *Running*, *Lightning*, and *Special Envoy*. His work has received a great number of literary prizes, among them the Prix Goncourt, the Prix Médicis, and the European Literature Jeopardy Prize. He lives in Paris.

MARK POLIZZOTTI has translated more than fifty books from the French, including Arthur Rimbaud's *The Drunken Boat: Selected Writings* (NYRB Poets), and is the author of twelve books, including *Revolution of the Mind: The Life of André Breton*, *Sympathy for the Traitor: A Translation Manifesto*, and *Why Surrealism Matters*. He lives in New York.

COMMAND PERFORMANCE

JEAN ECHENOZ

Translated from the French by
MARK POLIZZOTTI

NEW YORK REVIEW BOOKS

New York

THIS IS A NEW YORK REVIEW BOOK
PUBLISHED BY THE NEW YORK REVIEW OF BOOKS
207 East 32nd Street, New York, NY 10016
www.nyrb.com

**Albertine
Translation**

This work was awarded the Albertine Translation Prize in fiction/nonfiction
for excellence in publication and translation as part of Albertine Translation, a
program created by Villa Albertine and funded by FACE Foundation and the
Albertine Books Foundation with the support of Van Cleef & Arpels.

Command Performance was originally published by Les Éditions de Minuit as
Vie de Gérard Fulmard. Portions of chapters 35 and 36 have been revised for this
edition by the author in collaboration with the translator.

Library of Congress Cataloging-in-Publication Data
Names: Echenoz, Jean, author. | Polizzotti, Mark, translator.
Title: Command performance / a novel by Jean Echenoz; translated from the
   French by Mark Polizzotti.
Other titles: Vie de Gérard Fulmard. English
Identifiers: LCCN 2024010867 (print) | LCCN 2024010868 (ebook) | ISBN
   9781681378558 (paperback) | ISBN 9781681378565 (ebook)
Subjects: LCGFT: Novels.
Classification: LCC PQ2665.C5 V5413 2024 (print) | LCC PQ2665.C5 (ebook) |
   DDC 843/.914—dc23/eng/20240308
LC record available at https://lccn.loc.gov/2024010867
LC ebook record available at https://lccn.loc.gov/2024010868

ISBN 978-1-68137-855-8
Available as an electronic book; ISBN 978-1-68137-856-5

Printed in the United States of America on acid-free paper.
10 9 8 7 6 5 4 3 2 1

COMMAND PERFORMANCE

I

I WAS AT that point in my reflections when the disaster struck.

I know it's been much discussed, that it dragged many eyewitnesses out of the woodwork, spawned all manner of commentary and analysis, that its magnitude and uniqueness have enshrined it as a modern classic among news items. I know it's pointless and no doubt tedious to revisit the affair, but one of its repercussions I really do have to mention, as it concerns me personally, even if it's just a minor consequence.

Propelled at a speed of thirty yards per second, a huge bolt—the size of a hair dryer or clothes iron—hurtled through the window of an apartment on the fifth floor of a luxury building, shattering its glass and shredding its frame, and at the end of its trajectory, its point of impact was the owner of that apartment, a certain Robert D'Ortho, whose sternal region the bolt obliterated, causing instant death.

Certain other bolts confined themselves to material destruction, one crushing a parabolic antenna, another disemboweling the gateway of a residence located opposite the entrance to the shopping center. Those bolts could still be found scattered about, much later, in the course of investigations led by agents sporting hard hats and gloves and white coveralls. But these would be merely secondary effects, epiphenomena of the catastrophe that had just hit the superstore itself.

The condition of that hypermarket is, in fact, beyond hope. From the debris of its collapsed roof rises a fog of thick dust perforated by hesitant tongues of a burgeoning fire. The jagged, crenellated remains of its load-bearing walls expose their clawed steel beams, two of them leaning toward one another in a breach of equilibrium above the impact site. The glass of its facade, normally spangled with advertising notices, enticing offers, and smug slogans, is now striated from top to bottom and shattered at the corners. Standing before the reception area, three lampposts have collapsed into a group hug, intertwining their heads, whose sodium-vapor bulbs dangle from their sockets. Several cars, in the adjacent parking lot, have been overturned by the force of the blowback, others dimpled under the shock of flying objects, and behind their wipers twisted in parentheses, every windshield is missing.

Even though, as luck would have it, the tragedy occurred early in the morning, not long after the opening of the superstore, when crowds were still sparse, at first glance the human toll was probably not negligible: pending a precise estimate, and even as searches were being conducted in the disaster zone, the number of casualties could well have upset the public. The neighborhood was quickly sealed off, and in it were now gathered the forces of order and the EMTs, as well as bomb disposal technicians just in case, but not yet the army, and they hurriedly set up a psychological counseling tent. Since the first responders' efforts initially focused on the immediate area, it was only two days later that they discovered, on its outskirts, the body of Robert D'Ortho, perforated at home. And as I was saying, that's where I come in, for since this D'Ortho was the owner of, among other things, the two-and-a-half-room apartment where I reside, his demise would allow me to defer—if only temporarily—the payment of my monthly rent.

The event, then, unfolded not far from me; living three blocks away, I know the shopping center very well and often go there to stock up. It was around nine thirty. I was, as usual at that hour, dozing-slash-thinking about what I might do with my day, when the ruckus from the incident distracted me. At first I thought I could ignore it, then my attempts at reflection were frustrated by sirens, squawking police and rescue vehicles, as well as exclamations, cries, and shouts from all and sundry. But since curiosity is not my worst failing, I did not at first try to learn more.

Which can't be said of the crowds that immediately flooded the area: some fled the scene while others rushed in to get a look; people jostled each other, sometimes rather rudely, until the authorities came to add some shoving of their own, with no more understanding than anyone else of what had just happened. Since every sound and sight clearly suggested an explosion of some kind, the idea of a bomb and thus of a terrorist attack but also of a gas leak quickly took root: the populace waffled among mute shock, spontaneous com-mentary, and contradictory viewpoints. While the terrorist thesis initially held sway in public opinion, the rumor of an unexpected meteor collision then insinuated itself into the hive mind: such things happen, and examples are plentiful. Finally, the media got involved and announced that a huge chunk of obsolete Soviet satellite, on its return from infinite space, was what had demolished the Auteuil shopping cen-ter. Pieces of satellite fall to Earth nearly every day. And no one notices but the experts.

2

PUBLIC opinion underestimates such eventualities. This is understandable, given that astronautical detritus, which already tends to be rather small, further diminishes during its fall to Earth under the effects of friction, wear, and consumption in the dense layers of atmosphere. Ordinarily these scraps dissolve, and their negligible format, when not reduced to nothing, goes unremarked: public opinion takes little notice of them. On top of which, with seventy-five percent of Earth being covered in oceans, deserts, and inhospitable mountain ranges, there is only a slight risk that such fragments will fall onto a humanity that is increasingly agglutinated in cities.

Slight but not zero: a few did happen to come crashing down not too far from populations, albeit never—unless they're not telling us the whole truth—on those populations' heads. In recent years, for instance, without threatening life or limb, certain pieces smashed into the outskirts of Riyadh, near the well-heeled neighborhood of Georgetown, in the outer districts of Ankang, and in the middle of a park in Uganda. As for their nature, it is fairly diverse, sometimes consisting of simple straps, tiny paint chips, or eroded rivets, but also, more voluminously, of helium tanks, turbopumps, nozzles, docking air locks, or even whole exhausted rocket stages.

While we might be surprised that the fall of such wreckage has provoked so few deplorable accidents, we can also imagine them becoming more frequent. For, owing to the roughly five thousand launches since Sputnik 1 in 1957, there are approximately seven thousand tons of material currently orbiting the celestial vault above our craniums—filling our brains, in said craniums, with various data and, needless to say, facilitating the job of keeping tabs on our persons. Of the twenty thousand objects thus parading around, staring down at our orb, we can reasonably expect that three quarters of them, the ones gliding at less than a thousand kilometers of altitude, might well fall to Earth someday, somewhere or other, and why not at our feet. Let us note with relief that, past that distance, the life expectancy of the remaining quarter is a matter of centuries and might even aspire, in the extreme heights, to eternity.

Of course, it would be simple, or at least conceivable, to launch dedicated craft toward the ether, charged with eliminating the largest and most threatening detritus. As for the smaller pieces, we know that engineers, in their downtime, on their drawing boards, sketch out all sorts of hunting satellites equipped with harpoons, pincers, or nets with which to neutralize said detritus. Since the occupation of space can only escalate, this panoply of solutions should in principle prove indispensable, but, since this all costs a bundle, the relevant authorities pull a face. While that face is justified by the absence, so far, of homicidal impacts, and while it's true that the chances of being struck by a piece of space junk is sixty-five thousand times less (say the experts) than by lightning—still and all.

Still and all, the sad fact is that the second stage of an old Soviet Kosmos-3M launcher has just decimated my hypermarket. Previously, it had limped around in its orbit for more than half a century, alongside six hundred of its congeners expedited in mid–Cold War from bases in Plesetsk, Kapustin Yar, or Baikonur to install stealth military satellites in the heavens. And this launcher, even if many of its components flew off or melted during its fall, nonetheless weighed a good twenty tons when it tumbled down near my front door.

3

BACK TO me now. My name is Fulmard, first name Gerard, and I was born on May 13, 1974, in Gisors (Eure). Height: 5 ft 6 in. Weight: 196 lbs. Eyes: brown. Occupation: flight attendant. Residing on rue Erlanger, Paris 16th, where I live alone.

So, Gerard Fulmard, and while I have my share of disgruntlements, at least I'm not unhappy with that fairly uncommon family name, which doesn't sound at all bad and which is almost the name of a handsome seabird that I'd like to identify with, except that it's talkative and I, not so much. Except, too, that I don't share its physique, and in any event my excess embonpoint makes it unlikely I'll someday take flight. Even though, given my profession, I've also taken my fair share of flights, but first of all it's not the same thing, and besides, I'm no longer in the flight steward trade. My true current status is that of a job seeker looking to change occupations, but more on that later.

Apart from my name, I doubt I inspire much envy: I look like anyone else, only less so. Height slightly below average and weight slightly above, graceless physiognomy, education limited to a school equivalency certificate, social life and revenues approaching nil, family reduced to naught: I possess very few assets, advantages, or means. At least I was lucky enough to take over these two and a half rooms after my mother's passing; it was her lease and I didn't change the furniture. It's here that I'm now standing, windows ajar on a barely frequented street. It may be located in the Auteuil neighborhood, which contains primarily people of leisure, but the fact remains that rue Erlanger is not very cheery. I'll come back to that too.

Job seeker, as I said. Wishing to neither dwell forever in that category nor get used to it, I decided to start my own business, and even before clearly defining its purpose, I spent some time thinking up a company name. I occupied myself by making lists until I came up with the perfect moniker: Fulmard Assistance Bureau.

The name struck me as rather becoming. Lacking any special skill beyond serving meal trays at high altitude, I decided it was in my interest to portray myself in the most diffuse light possible: hopefully the light would conceal the lack. In that regard, the term "assistance" casts a wide net and commits me to nothing. From accounting to plumbing to personal development, domains into which I'll never venture, assistance is all-purpose: it's the ideal label, whose polysemy allows for anything and everything. That settled, I still had to define my project. I blew some of the three cents I'd put aside on doing what, it seemed to me, one should do in such circumstances: placing an ad to announce my arrival on the market, with a view toward sticking a plaque on my door.

The plaque I'd soon take care of. The ad I placed on the cheap in one of those free papers that poor people hand out to other poor people at metro exits. With those two pillars underway, all I had to do was wait. Determined, open to any offers, I waited calmly: you'll hear tell of Gerard Fulmard, you'll come to know the Fulmard Assistance Bureau. Until then, as my three cents had dwindled to just one, I blessed the heavens and especially what had just fallen from them onto Auteuil, thanks to which my rent payment could wait.

But why, you might ask, am I no longer a flight attendant, no longer in such an enviable profession? Well, without mentioning the handicap of my excess weight, somewhat frowned upon in aviation circles, let's just say I practiced it for six years before being let go for cause. I won't elaborate on that cause, other than to say it earned me a suspended sentence and obligatory therapy. Thus obliged, I go two Tuesday mornings a month to a prescribed medical facility located on rue du Louvre; my treatment consists of mono-loguing to the half-closed eyes of a psychiatrist named Jean-François Bardot. I suspect this Bardot of holding such legally mandated sessions with the sole aim of feeding the kitty, further buttering the bread that—judging from his tailored suits and his Audi Q2 parked in front of the building—he must earn in pretty thick slices in private practice. Whatever the case, I tell him about my life without lying more than one time in three, lay out my plans to rejoin society, which he approves and encourages monosyllabically, though I sus-pect without really listening to them. I mostly get the im-pression he couldn't care less.

If I'm telling you this, it's because it's related to my proj-ect, at least tangentially, as we'll see. It so happens that the facility where I get treated is next door to an establishment, also located on rue du Louvre, whose sign proclaims in mint-green neon the words DULUC DETECTIVE, which attract attention and to which no soul with even the slightest sense of romance, mine included, could possibly remain indiffer-ent. This establishment is quite familiar to passersby, it is part of the Parisian landscape, it injects a touch of adventure, however outmoded: you even see it in films, the titles of which escape me, but let's get down to the facts.

It was there, strolling past Duluc's as I left Bardot's, that my entrepreneurial objective became clarified. As my eyes met the green neon, Why not, I asked myself, go into that line of work? After all, stewardship had trained me in human contact, I was interested in all sorts of things, and my bland physiognomy could work in my favor. Besides, my enforced idleness, since being shown the door, left me ample time to read and see abundant novels and films of the genre that often focused on the role of investigator, with which I'd thereby become familiar.

I realize this is a very common notion, one that has crossed everyone's mind at some point. Who hasn't fantasized about solving a mystery, clearing up a drama, or righting wrongs, restoring the orphan to his heritage, or having it off with the widow on the fly? It has become so commonplace that we no longer dare imagine it, even in one of those novels I've read, but maybe that's precisely its strength. For the banality of this role, too overused and threadbare to be true, must be off-putting to the average Joe, must attract few applicants, so why not Gerard Fulmard? And besides, it's not all hunting down serial killers, international spies, runaway heiresses, and other gripping exploits. There must also be less glamorous investigations—insurance fraud, extra-conjugal imbroglios, locating a deadbeat—that make you a kind of private bailiff. It's humble, certainly. Even thankless. But it might pay. That's for me.

And so I made my decision and I wrote my ad: FULMARD ASSISTANCE BUREAU, INFORMATION & QUERIES, DISPUTES & DEBT COLLECTION, PROMPTNESS & DISCRETION. At the foot of those substantives, I placed my telephone number and address, then I rushed off to deliver it to the editorial office of the free paper.

And now I wait. Lying on my bed, I build castles in the air. I compose a gruff yet empathetic manner with which to greet my clientele. If said clientele proves abundant, I could easily transform my half room into a waiting area. I wonder about carrying a piece, as well as about sexual opportunities. Following a train of thought, I envision hiring a secretary. I tremble as I imagine the recruiting process. I think about all this, and a few of these thoughts I might mention to Jean-François Bardot, but not all of them.

4

So I WAS at that point in my ruminations when the phenomenon occurred: extreme commotion coming from not far away, almost immediately followed by screeches, wails, hues and cries. I smelled a serious news item, the kind that the TV blares out urgently. I got up to turn on my set, lay back down to watch it, waited a moment, and it wasn't long in coming, interrupting our program: a news flash relating that a hunk of aerospace had just ruined an edifice only three hundred yards from my bed, from which, nonetheless, I did not move.

I could have thrown on some clothes and run to see what was happening, but there must already have been a plethora of bodies out there in the late November chill, and, given my short stature, over the shoulders of that plethora I would no doubt catch only the flu. I preferred to follow the developments on television, for disasters are like sporting events, and more generally like everything else: on-screen is better than on-site, you get a clearer picture of the overall effects and details of the action, and close-ups following slow-motion shots are intercut with recaps to enlighten the viewer. Most of all, you avoid stampedes, the jostling and promiscuity favored by siphoners of wallets and sexual gropers—even if I'm not the ideal prey in the eyes of such predators, the former and still less the latter.

After the news flash with its blaring headlines, having nothing more to say, they went back to their usual morning programming: pointers on health, cooking, culture, well-being, and other instructive things, and I was able to grab a bit more sleep. Then another headline, less vivacious but more insinuating—ingratiating violins over anxiogenic bass—wrenched me from the beginning of a rather sweet dream in the company of my virtual secretary: a special broadcast devoted to the Auteuil disaster.

The latter was summarized, developed, commented on by various scientists, military men, experts of all stripes who had been summoned in extremis, with, as always, two or three politicos representing minor organizations—the major ones not having bothered—and I recognized two of them. The one named Bernard Couplet, a deputy in the MDM (Movement for Democratic Momentum), in a slate-colored suit and tie, blandly admitted the hazards presented by our technological progress, whose benefits he nonetheless listed, identifying with the grief of the families and invoking public solidarity. He's not very exciting, Couplet, hardly charismatic, his rhetoric is so flaccid that it smothers his points.

The second one, on the other hand, Joel Chanelle, always gets more notice because he is scrappy, his vocabulary virulent and crude, his morphology round and shiny, his tie bright green, and his jacket less fitted. Lacking an electoral mandate, but serving as a spokesperson for Franck Terrail—chairman of the IPF (Independent Popular Federation), of which Chanelle is also the director general—he profited from the situation to mount an attack. Let's stop trying to make the French people believe nonsense, he shouted, before presenting the disaster as a direct consequence of the permissive, elitist, laxist ideology conveyed by the so-called democratic momentum, then attacking Couplet himself via allusions to his private life, hinting at a few intimate details about which, he continued with a smirk, it was best not to say too much. Bernard Couplet at first feigned indifference, then fired off what he thought was a devastating comeback that in fact no one understood: Given some of your friends, such as Mr. Mozzigonacci, he murmured insinuatingly, our democracy had better watch out. Seeing that his low blow had failed to land, he then tried indignation, hoping to make a splash, and, solemnly rising from his seat, he stalked off the set live on camera. It might have had some small effect, but, since the camera was on Chanelle at the time and Couplet's mic had fallen off when he stood up, no one noticed.

From that point, apparently unconcerned about straying off topic, Chanelle deployed his digressions on various themes. Referring as quickly as possible to the thinking of Chairman Terrail, he ventured, with what amounted to exaltation, on to family values, which didn't have much to do with the calamity at hand but allowed him to renew his homage to Franck Terrail; his partner, Nicole Tourneur; as well as his stepdaughter, Louise Tourneur. Must I remind you that Nicole Tourneur does not merely share the chairman's bed, but also is national secretary of the Independent Popular Federation?

They gave the floor back to the experts, who had begun arguing among themselves, their exchanges rhythmically intercut with live sequences: eyewitness interviews (I recognized one of the girls who worked at reception at the shopping center), the reaction of the interior minister, recollections from astronauts, early forecasts from opinion pollsters. An update on the situation in Auteuil was effected every fifteen minutes by an intern against a background of smoking rubble, while another intern cooled his heels in front of the Russian embassy. Then the soundstage was refreshed: while they were at it, they brought in philosophers, clergy, and a few millenarians; there was even a euhemerist druid in full dress yelling that nothing ever changed, he had shouted his guts out warning of a catastrophe and no one had listened.

The whole thing was naturally punctuated by ads of all sorts—for dream cruises, phenomenal detergent, a fantabulous stair lift—the announcers having tripled their prices on the occasion of this affair, and, as it was beginning to drag on, I hopped from channel to channel until I found a suitable documentary. Now, said documentary—at first innocently about nature but then positing the extinction in the medium term of both Asian and African elephants—went on to anticipate the disappearance of all animals, of smaller and smaller sizes and in the more or less long term. It, too, was set to conclude on a note of calamity, and I became weary and then unconscious.

5

My slumber didn't last long. No sooner had my secretary reentered than another news flash tore me away from her lips, blaring even more ear-splittingly from the radio, announcing another special broadcast but on a different topic.

It seems to me that news flashes rarely follow each other in such rapid succession. I have no authority over this, but if you don't mind my saying so, they shouldn't be allowed to become so systematic, or people won't have time to catch their breath. Not counting the fact that the producers, directors, and announcers of run-of-the-mill news broadcasts might take offense and threaten to go on strike, which could lead to social unrest and the possible risk of urban violence, which would entail more special reports, and it could go on that way forever.

But anyway, I watched. This particular broadcast opened without preamble on a video clip. We saw a good-looking woman, well into her fifties, who appeared carelessly dressed— greenish hoodie over brown T-shirt—framed head-to-bust and facing the camera; she was reciting something and reminded me of someone. Shaky camera, harsh lighting: clearly amateur work. The woman seemed to be reading the text she was reciting, for her eyes constantly flickered away as if to check a teleprompter, and her voice was monotonous and wobbly. As for the someone she reminded me of, this so absorbed my attention that at first I didn't grasp what she was saying. Finally, more than her face, it was the head-to-bust framing, especially the bust itself, that, having drawn my gaze, finally clued me in. I recognized her, I had seen her on TV but in other contexts: despite her lack of makeup and blow-dry, it was surely Nicole Tourneur, national secretary of the Independent Popular Federation and second wife of its chairman, Franck Terrail, mentioned earlier, during the debate about Auteuil.

Incidentally, why Nicole Tourneur kept her maiden name, unless it was the name of her first husband, no one knows, and it's none of my business. We sometimes observe this phenomenon with certain women who become public figures: they might get remarried ten times over, but they're obliged to keep their former name; otherwise, they'd have to start from scratch, but never mind.

The video ended. Long shot of another soundstage, successive close-ups of the guests that the host named one by one. Scientists, servicemen, philosophers, and druids had vanished, replaced by two leading journalists and a few politicians I didn't recognize, except for Joel Chanelle, still in the foreground and having merely changed seats. At this rate, going from one special report to the next, Chanelle should have been exhausted, at least I would have been in his shoes, but on the contrary, he looked to be in even finer fettle than before. Since the current situation—in other words, the kidnapping, if I'd understood correctly, of his national secretary—concerned him deeply, it should have incited even more pugnacious comments than during the preceding debate about the Auteuil tragedy, which presumably would elicit a collective grief. But again, on the contrary: the kidnapping, which seemed to be politically motivated—

Nicole Tourneur being a notable figure in that sphere—called for serious unanimity. Chanelle, despite his phenomenal energy, adopted a sober, dignified register, draping himself in a pose of lofty outrage.

Rebroadcast of the video for those, the host clarified, who had just joined us. This time, I listened more carefully to what Mother Tourneur had to say. It seemed from her remarks that she was being held by a group whose nature and goals struck me as muddled, their demands elliptical, and their ideology murky, but who seemed to leave the door open to negotiations, the nature of which would be specified in a future communiqué. The whole thing seemed rather vague, unless my analysis was faulty.

I have to confess that Nicole Tourneur really isn't bad-looking for her age, the mature type that I wouldn't turn up my nose at; she'll do in a pinch. Even though when it comes to a different, somewhat fresher type, I feel a much keener liking for her daughter, Louise Tourneur, whom we also sometimes see on television, as she also plays a small role in the IPF. Something like a media consultant, as she seems to like to communicate as much as possible, though she wasn't onstage now, and I greatly deplored her absence. Of course, under the circumstances, I naturally understood that she had other things on her mind, but I regretted it all the same, as there's nothing to dislike about Louise Tourneur. Her entire person delights me, point for point. Eyes, face, bearing, smile. Outline, affiliations, elegance, shape. Presence, distinction, voice. But enough about me.

6

SOMETIMES I just can't take it anymore, Ermosthenes mutters in lament. Stay focused, murmurs Apollodore.

Not far away, alone and nude, Louise Tourneur swims back and forth in a pool twenty yards by twelve. In the background stands a modern, convoluted villa: recesses and overhangs, polychrome picture windows, cockleshell bartizans, asymptotic balustrades, and other fancies.

The swimming pool is bordered along its width by giant potted cacti; along one length, a vegetal barrier composed of a row of voluminous agaves shields it from prying eyes. Around the pool spreads a terrace of skid-resistant marble punctuated by glazed jars in which grow *Melianthus major* or *Fatsia japonica*. Armchairs made of hemp fiber, deck chairs in black lizard skin, and coffee tables in bubinga delimit a summer salon around a serving cart supporting alcoholic beverages of varying strengths, soft drinks, and energy drinks, with an ice bucket of hand-embossed vermeil, on the flank of which the sun now gently poses a prurient reflection. We are among the rich, the weather is fine.

On the margins of the terrace, in an adjacent space reserved for staff, the brothers Apollodore and Ermosthenes Nguyen are squaring off around a go board: they're endeavoring to replay the famous match known as "the ear-reddening game," which pitted Honinbo Shusaku (black) against Inoue Genan

Inseki (white) in Osaka, from the eleventh to the fifteenth of September 1846. Although absorbed in their match, the Nguyen brothers regularly cast brief circular glances around the perimeter, since they enjoy, vis-à-vis the swimmer, the status of bodyguards. A body that the guards are under orders both to turn away from as long as it is unclothed—which seems to be distressing Ermosthenes—and to ensure that no intruder covertly observes in its displacements.

From end to end, Louise Tourneur thus comes and goes in that pool tiled in bricks of molten glass that evolve through every shade of blue, from cobalt to sky. Her rhythm is reasonable but sustained. Between outbounds in crawl and inbounds in racing breaststroke, one can alternately make out her face in profile or head-on. She proceeds without straining, neither getting short of breath nor overly taxing her muscles for a length of twenty-four hundred yards, a middle distance that she imposes on herself every morning.

Seeing her swim, we can understand Gerard Fulmard's enthusiasm, as Louise Tourneur's anatomy—blurred by the waves, prolonged by the wake, festooned by foam—does appear slender, long-limbed, harmonious, and all the better proportioned in that movement flatters such attributes. Her 120 laps accomplished, as she rises from the water, naked in the open air, hoisting herself on the bars of the ladder while shaking her hair, we see her all the better.

At which point we find ourselves growing a tad disillusioned, for all things considered, let's be honest, Fulmard got carried away: Louise Tourneur is admittedly not bad, but not as good as all that. Even if she incarnates a standard model of a tall, slim, tanned blond with well-calibrated curves, her chin is a bit too angular, she has mild strabismus in her left eye, her feet are not terribly trim, little things like that. Still, let's not go too far in the other direction, let's recognize that she has allure, just not to the degree imagined by Gerard—who, moreover, has never seen her except put together on screen, photoshopped in magazines, or retouched on posters, which can be more forgiving.

At that point, there appears at the other end of the pool—coming sufficiently from out of nowhere to elude the vigilance of the Nguyen brothers—a fellow, thirty years old, who is also blond but sports white trousers, a yellow jacket, and a pale carnation, and has wide shoulders. Louise Tourneur knows this fellow slightly, Guillaume Flax, she was introduced to him when he was a rising young star in the IPF. But star-like as he seemed, Flax ultimately did no more than seem: his star soon fell, before flaming out altogether and morphing into a mere satellite of Joel Chanelle, the sun of the party of which Flax is no more than a secondary ray, his role now limited to coordinating among sections under the supervision of Cedric Ballester—who is himself, as we shall see, an altogether more promising luminary in the party's org chart.

In any case, here's young Flax, with a dopey smile, taking in the view until Louise Tourneur notices his presence. As Louise's robe is folded over a lounge chair several yards away, she looks around for a bath towel, all the while displaying a pout of offended modesty—there's never any peace, the Nguyens are going to hear about this. But Flax has already stridden to the lounge chair and snatched up the robe, which he holds out, albeit from far enough away to oblige the still-naked young woman to take two steps toward him to grab it.

I just wanted to let you know, says Flax as she belts the garment, Franck is asking for you. He could have called me directly, Louise Tourneur frowns. I don't think you had your phone on you at the time, Flax insinuates. Franck told me to hurry, so I'm hurrying. But hurried as he claims to be, and despite the mission accomplished, Flax doesn't seem eager to leave.

After a long latency period, owing to a territorial dispute in the lower right corner of the *goban*, the Nguyens finally appear. Louise Tourneur having shot them two brief movements of eye and chin, Apollodore Nguyen politely grips Guillaume Flax's left elbow, Ermosthenes firmly grips his right shoulder, and they accompany him to the exit with enough vigor that Flax, momentarily thrown off balance, nearly stumbles over the initial agave. Louise Tourneur has not been watching the trio leave: from her sullen way of toweling her hair, straightening her lopsided robe, and trying several times to light a cigarette, we can infer that she is peeved.

She crosses the terrace toward the villa and goes up to her room, where she showers, quickly puts on makeup, then dresses more slowly, hesitating on the one hand among three tops, and on the other among the reasons Franck Terrail might have for summoning her. Then she goes back outside and heads for another villa three hundred yards away, architecturally congruent and housing Dorothée Lopez. Louise Tourneur knows Dorothée Lopez well enough to drop in unannounced.

Having entered without knocking, she crosses the foyer toward a living room where, a phone glued to each ear, Dorothée Lopez seems to be holding two agitated conversations simultaneously, standing in front of her television, on whose screen Louise Tourneur notices Nicole Tourneur, facing the camera, dressed in unfamiliar clothes, making unfamiliar statements in an unfamiliar tone of voice, and Louise's eyes widen. What's my mother doing in there? she thinks. Then she asks the same of Dorothée.

7

THE LIVING room in Dorothée Lopez's house bespeaks the same affluence as Louise Tourneur's summer salon near her pool, but larger and better adapted to the additional three seasons. The carpets and furnishings—console tables stratified with art books and auction catalogs, méridiennes, sofas, poufs—as well as the decoration—a Staël, a Klein, three antiquities on plinths—denote analogous tastes and bankrolls.

The setting is more or less the same in the dozen opulent habitations, neighboring those of Lopez and Tourneur, that form a residential complex, closed, private, autonomous, and removed from urban interactions: everything is designed to ensure the owners' peace and quiet. Somewhere between the La Muette and Sablons neighborhoods, its address is more-over so hidden, so secret, that even here we cannot disclose it more precisely.

Such an ensemble is not unique in its genre. There exist others in Paris and its environs, such as the Villa Montmorency, the hamlet of Boulainvilliers, and the Maisons-Laffitte park, but these are less closely observed. This one—encircled by ten-foot-high vegetation-covered walls bristling with infrared sensors, thermal cameras, and other detectors of motion, odor, breath, and heartbeat—is entered via a deterrent chicane and a gate with a double grille, an electronic code, and a sworn sentry in a booth, before one ventures forth beneath a host of video-surveillant gazes.

The complex was built some twenty years ago, on the grounds of an old allotment energetically expropriated beneath the expensively averted gaze of the planning commission. At the time of its conception, following Oscar Newman's theses on defensible space, the roadways were reconfigured: blocking off the old, grid-like streets and transforming them into cul-de-sacs reduced traffic flow, while making it easier to watch comings, goings, entrances, and exits during regular rounds by patrols with bullmastiffs around the residences, which are themselves equipped with a continually refreshed technological arsenal—multifunctional glazing, central units, automated controls.

All the inhabitants of this fortified enclave know one another, resemble one another, surround themselves with their peers in a tribal mode of co-optation, such that their homes and hearths also resemble one another, aside from one or two external signs of wealth: Paul Newman's Daytona, Bugatti Veyron Super Sport, or Cy Twombly. While each enjoys his or her own swimming pool and home cinema, a shared gym and tennis court mark their solidarity. In the same way, by turns, depending on each resident's talents and tastes, a collective agreement provides that each shall be responsible for an aspect of bunker life.

For as we well know, a feature of the privileged is that they band together: their goal is social security, capital promotes inter se. And while competition initially encouraged them to jostle and trample one another in a frantic free-for-all, now that their fortunes have been made, they opt for a collective real estate that they alone maintain. This community of interests strikes them as nothing less than salubrious. Crushing in elbow to elbow without compromising their freedom of action, they share the tasks: as such, one presides over the landscaping in his off moments, another the administrative chores, yet another the computerized monitoring systems. As for the recruitment of personnel—maintenance staff, gardeners, guards, servants—it is handled by Dorothée Lopez: to her we owe, for instance, after tests, preliminary interviews, and a trial period, the hiring—with a term limit—of the Nguyen brothers.

Dorothée Lopez: lawyer with the Paris bar; consultant for the IPF and close associate of its leaders; tall, svelte fifty-something with reddish locks, dressed in light, floating fabrics in matching shades. She continues to talk nervously into her two telephones, and no doubt she is speaking, in this moment of crisis, to two operatives of the party whose national secretary is still making her statement in a static shot. When this shot comes to an end, the day's news regains pride of place, our special correspondent on the scene gives the updated toll from the Auteuil disaster, and Lopez turns off her phones and her television, muttering they're a pain in the ass with their disasters.

When Louise Tourneur again asks what her mother is doing there, Dorothée Lopez helps her understand that she seems to be in a bad situation: I've been trying to reach Chanelle, we can't just sit on our hands, we have to issue a press release, but nothing doing, all I get is his voicemail or useless nitwits. Somebody has to, I don't know. Ballester? suggests Louise Tourneur. No, Lopez interrupts her, Cedric is too young to manage this. I assume Franck knows about it? Louise Tourneur supposes. Don't talk to me about Franck, exhales Lopez, he's even worse than usual. Franck is in terrible shape, we can't rely on him.

Franck: Franck Terrail, sixty-eight, nth husband of Nicole Tourneur, founding chairman of the IPF, though his status is now purely honorific. A trained historian, he has gone back to his research and spends his time on that. No longer attends party congresses, annual conferences, and summer sessions, except for appearances' sake, and never says anything of consequence. Increasingly delegates power of decision to Joel Chanelle.

A pause. They reflect. Cinnamon tea, Japanese biscuits, rumble of a Koenigsegg Agera V8 bi-turbo engine along a drive path, cheeping of crows and swifts.

That said, Dorothée Lopez ventures, you could try to talk to him yourself, to Franck—he is your stepfather, after all, and he'll listen to you. Louise hedges that she'll have to see, we'll have to see, she'll see. I get it, sighs Lopez, anyway, Franck really only listens to Luigi. Luigi Pannone, you know who I mean? Of course I know. Louise Tourneur's eyes—green—roll to the sky. Fine, Lopez abbreviates, I'm going to try to draft a communiqué until I can reach Joel. If it takes too long, I'll send young Flax. Or else Cedric, of course.

Cedric: Cedric Ballester, thirty-two, parliamentary adjunct to Joel Chanelle. A handsome brunet with long eyelashes, deep-set eyes, meaty lips, and long teeth, Cedric Ballester is the type who chases anything that moves, sex, power, or both. With Lopez he was able to deploy his talents: she remembers in detail the evening when he got around her, seduced her, penetrated her from three angles, and dropped her, in three hours. She has forgiven him. Let's forget it.

Let's forget it, because someone is at the door and Dorothée Lopez is going to see who it is. Louise Tourneur hears her speaking with the older of the Nguyens, who has come to apologize for their delay in reacting, he and his brother, earlier, at the poolside. And if Madame Lopez would be so good as to speak to Miss Tourneur so that the latter will not hold it against them, etc. Lopez abridges, promises, returns while grumbling that you never get left in peace, anyway, what were we talking about?

8

Let us come back, a few days later, to me, still putting together my project.

Secretary-wise, I quit daydreaming, deferred my hiring plans—on top of which I was studying the profiles of potential candidates, less in the files of employment agencies than, for lack of better, in the glossy pages of specialized periodicals distributed with onanistic intent, for no two ways about it, Gerard Fulmard's sex life was surplus goods. But patience, let's not be hasty, we'll consider this abstinence fuel for my project, let us even posit that a rational asceticism incites one to concentrate more acutely on the future.

Meanwhile, two days earlier I'd mentioned my entrepreneurial plans to Dr. Bardot. He didn't react, not even to encourage me, perhaps he didn't understand or, go figure, wasn't listening. More and more I get the feeling that he really doesn't give a crap.

For the moment, the registered address of my business is, no surprise, rue Erlanger. I've already hinted that rue Erlanger is not terribly lively; sometimes nothing is as gloomy, especially on a Sunday, as its sixteen hundred by forty feet, its meager traffic, and its total of four shops: an Asian massage parlor, a mobile phone pop-up, a seller of "smart" aquabike systems, and a nail salon. There is also, of course, a grocery store at one end, but its prices are way above the Fulmard index. So shopping has become a real hassle since the Soviet detritus made away with our hypermarket.

My home office, then, as it currently stands: these two and a half rooms. And as I still lack the means for a genuine engraved plaque, with the help of a Dymo label maker I affixed to the door the logo FAB, followed by the words ENTER AFTER RINGING. Those initials tickle me. I find them more stylish than the full title; they give you a slightly anonymous character, initiatory and chic, a bit Anglo, which I like: the Fulmard Assistance Bureau has now been launched onto the market.

Regarding the layout, I indeed transformed my half room into a waiting area, furnished with three chairs and isolated from my office by a pine-green reinforced plastic partition with accordion folds that squeak but that's okay, and in fact is all the more okay in that for now there are precious few clients. Since I can only wait, and since hygiene inspires confidence, I proceeded to deep-clean the premises: swept, dusted, washed windows following advice I'd picked up in the giveaway where I placed my ad, crumpling its own pages, which I'd moistened with white vinegar. I then deposited other giveaways on one of the chairs, accompanied by magazines that I sometimes confiscate when they jut out from the tenants' mailboxes and, as far as I'm concerned, make the place look messy. Order thus reigns in the lobby, and if the neighbors were to complain about these pilferings, logically they should be my first clients: I'd gladly represent their interests. Now that everything is clean, I watch and wait.

It has now been five days that I've been watching and waiting at my workstation, furnished with a narrow metal locker and my mother's two armchairs facing my desk, behind which, in a third chair retrieved from the sidewalk, I sit. I sit, leafing through my neighbors' magazines, once I've rolled into a ball their translucent wrappers that alone populate—temporarily, I tell myself—my wastepaper basket.

My desk is just a plank on sawhorses, whose severity I softened with a Bulgomme carpet, on which rest a lamp, a ledger, a notepad, and an ashtray. Plus the metal locker, the kind you see in gymnasium changing rooms and which will presumably soon buckle under the weight of my clients' files; for the moment, I store in it, in the upper, locked compartment, only the specialized magazines previously mentioned. As for wall decorations, I've opted for sobriety: hanging behind me is a framed engineering diploma, found in a thrift store, and from which I scraped off the name of a certain François Floquet and substituted that of Gerard Fulmard, nothing more.

I'd been ready since Monday. It was now Friday and, through my pine-colored folding screen, I heard someone finally ring, enter, and sit down. I was careful not to leap onto the new arrival, taking time to assume the demeanor of a professional who has other things to do. Feigning a telephone call, loud enough for the client to overhear and be impressed by, I flung into the void some purely random high figures, tossed out one or two famous names along with the four words of English I knew.

Finally standing up, I folded back the partition and looked over the man, in a tight zinc-gray suit and shirt buttoned to his glottis, who happened to be my first client. He looked kind of old; his cheeks were pasty and purplish, his bald pate the color of suet, not attractive. I ushered him into my office with a somber look, and once we were sitting opposite each other, I pretended to feel my cell phone vibrate: raising my index finger as a sign to wait, I emitted with annoyance two sentences of general interest with the tone of ridding myself of a serious nuisance. After which I simulated verifying something in my ledger, whose virginity I concealed. Remaining pensive, as if in the middle of a crucial decision, I finally appeared to discover the presence of the oldster and how can I help you, I said.

Even to a neophyte like me, his case seemed simple: his wife had disappeared, he blurted out, and I was careful not to show how much I sympathized with her. I grabbed my notepad and a ballpoint to jot down what he was saying, but my ballpoint was dry: I vainly scratched at the pad, which tore with a smudge. As I saw the old man watching, I took another tack: I paused a moment, put away the Bic, and pretended to adapt my method to his specific case. In this type of situation, I expounded, I'd rather not write anything down for now. I prefer, I elaborated, that our verbal interaction be combined with a visual exchange, don't you see, that this first conversation passes, so to speak, through a sort of *scopic* bargain—I don't know how I managed to come up with all that, but in any case the oldster nodded vigorously. That is how I work, I brazenly concluded.

The old man seemed bowled over by this problematic: first he bit, then he poured it out. His wife, or more precisely, let's say, his protégée—he must have been a widower who'd hooked up with a young thing: major blunder—had vanished the day before yesterday. He had seen my ad in the free newspaper and there you had it. Right, I uttered. Has she taken her things? Did she have any friends? You hadn't noticed any signs? Did you have a fight? No, the old man answered each time. And her name is Janine. Maybe not as young as all that, I deduced in my heart of hearts.

Once he had unpacked his little tale, I immediately dramatized matters in order to raise the stakes and therefore the price. The situation seems serious, I diagnosed, no doubt more than you realize. We must act in greatest haste. Swearing to dive into the case forthwith, I held my breath and indicated my honorarium: two hundred euros a day plus expenses.

I've never entirely understood what exactly is meant by *plus expenses*, a syntagm garnered from genre publications, but I suppose it designates taxis, metro tickets—in my case, especially metro tickets—aperitifs needed for research, that sort of thing; in any event, I intended to cram as many charges as possible into that niche. The oldster consented blindly, and I should have asked for three-fifty, but the damage was done.

Though I now knew Janine's first name, I realized that I had not asked my client *his* name, which wasn't very professional, and I was afraid he'd grow suspicious. Since the dryness of my ballpoint—I didn't have a spare—prevented me from noting his identity, I found a way to justify this via another risky concept: Initial anonymity is precious compost, I assured him with a benevolent smile—no doubt about it, I was in an inventive mood. As he smiled back shyly, I added that that would be all for today, as I had to reflect, not knowing what else to say to him in truth other than to give the fee for our conversation that day: Eighty euros, please. He again agreed and everything was going great and I found myself to be quite good at this. Can I write you a check, he proposed. I gladly concurred. After he had paid without quibbling, I set an appointment for the next day to study the matter more closely. And for him to thereby pay me more abundantly.

Supposedly reflecting after his departure, it took little time for me to admit that reflection was not in my skill set. Perhaps the emotion of having my first client. I pretended to straighten my papers, but as I had but few papers, and since there's no point in pretending for yourself, I took a spin around the waiting area to stretch my legs. There I picked up a regular newspaper, no doubt left there by the oldster, and leafing through it I learned that the secretary of the Independent Popular Federation was still missing. They were waiting for her kidnappers to make their demands, there was concern in high places. They were waiting for an official reaction from her spouse, Franck Terrail, who was to speak at a specially convened meeting. They were waiting for the date and time of this meeting to be announced. They were waiting, it seemed, for a fair number of things, which was understandable. I decided to wait as well.

9

IT'S IN a yellow Honda roadster, an earpiece wedged in his left auricle, that Luigi Pannone is driving above the prescribed speed limit on the inner beltway, near Porte Brancion, heading west. His hands are damp, his brow knitted, his nose straddled by polarized lenses that protect him from a sun whose rays are stretching their limbs before going to bed.

Luigi Pannone is a thin, dry subject of average height and razorlike profile, cinched in a belted blazer, coiffed with hair gel, and endowed with a narrow line of mustache traced in charcoal. Officially an asset manager, Pannone is especially a fixture of the Independent Popular Federation, the assets he manages being primarily those, intellectual and moral, of Franck Terrail, whose number one assistant he is.

A former Turinese executive in the Italian Social Movement, from which he defected after the transformations of 1995, Pannone had had to leave Piedmont to settle in France, where, at first a basic militant within the IPF, he rose in its ranks to end up in the exclusive service of Chairman Terrail. Now his counsel, his confidant, occasionally his cook, he devotedly handles everything requiring a practical sense, with which Franck Terrail is poorly endowed.

As he exits the beltway at Porte de Sèvres before impetuously zipping down rue Balard, his car radio offers him a synthesis of what we already know, for now, about the kidnapping of Nicole Tourneur. Pannone turns up the volume to maximum, then immediately lowers it, for, via his earpiece, he knows more than the news media. Reaching Quai André Citroën, he follows the Left Bank of the river for three hundred yards before reaching the tall constructions of the Front de Seine, at the foot of which, while parking haphazardly, he spots a Havana-brown Audi Q2 speeding off: Pannone identifies it, Pannone grimaces, thinking about the treatments—psychological, electric, and intravenous—that they inflict on Terrail every God-given day, not to mention all the tests he has to undergo. It's in quickstep that he then reaches Nelson Towers, whose express elevator lifts him to the twenty-second floor, right hallway, second door on the right, to which Luigi Pannone, a trusted figure, holds a duplicate key.

Crossing the threshold, Pannone glances toward the empty living room, blinks at each bedroom, then heads toward the study, knocks on the door, and, getting no reply, he delicately turns the knob. It is a huge but dark room. The lowered blinds barely leave visible the walls lined with overstuffed bookcases; a work surface with drawers and shelves laden with papers, files, and books; an equally ballasted lectern; and two armchairs framing a couch, on which a supine Franck Terrail half opens a gluey eye.

Unshaven, uncombed, wan, in a loosely knotted bathrobe, the chairman of the IPF does not seem in tip-top shape. He is holding documents of small format, apparently contained in a bound octavo anthology of Augustan poets, which he immediately shuts. Are you okay, Franck? Pannone gently inquires. Terrail barely rises, slides the anthology under the couch, then, stretching out again: Not really, he utters pastily, I feel like I've lost all my strength.

Franck, again: top schools, history degree, author of a standard reference work entitled *Power and Prestige of the Local Elites in Egypt During the First Intermediate Period (Late Third Millennium BC)* and published by Perrin in a condensed edition; this man, who is not exactly a tribune, hardly seemed predisposed to political life. A speculative intellectual, not terribly sociable, preferring solitary writing to tumultuous oration, Franck Terrail is neither effusive nor talkative, not the sort of man to run a campaign and press the flesh in the market on a Sunday: he likes neither Sundays nor markets nor pressing anything at all. On top of which, chronically indecisive when called upon to arbitrate, dubious of any option, he readily cloisters himself in an all-purpose skeptical reticence, ill suited to the styles associated with power. No, he wasn't made for this, still less in that his mood often veers toward despondency.

Luigi Pannone raises the blinds, lifting his eyes to the sky, which he finds thus: bright, clear, close to dusk. Pannone is accustomed to this mood of Franck's, inured to its effects, aware of his boss's weaknesses. When these bouts occur, Pannone knows that he turns to various therapists, discreetly chosen from within the party ranks. So did you see the doctor, Franck? he asks. What doctor? mutters Terrail. The shrink, Pannone specifies. Ah, right, Terrail grumbles, he's a moron. And did you manage to get some sleep? Pannone asks again. Did you eat anything? Nothing, murmurs Terrail. Haven't had a bite in days.

Understandable, with everything going on, Pannone permits himself to comment. As Terrail asks what's going on, Pannone chooses not to reply. This is not working, he thinks, then articulates in a firm voice: There's a lot we need to do. You're weak, the body languishes without sustenance, I'm going to make you orecchiette the way I know you like. Some nice little orecchiette with anchovies and turnip shoots, no? Luigi's nice little orecchiette? If you want, sighs Terrail, getting up very slowly. Oh, on second thought, no, just an egg, that'll do.

I'll go take a leak in the meantime, Franck states dreamily. Hardly has he left the room than Luigi Pannone rushes to the couch, squats, slides toward him the Augustan volume, which he opens, pulls out the documents that Terrail was studying, and: Bloody hell, Pannone shudders, this is all we needed.

They are photographs, a dozen in number. They all depict the same person, to wit, Louise Tourneur, from various angles but with one point in common: she is at least as naked as the other day in the pool. From their improvised framing, one infers that they were taken in haste and without the young woman's knowledge; from their rumpled state, one also infers that they have been much looked at, much manipulated. Pannone remains squatting for a moment to flip through them one by one, so focused that he notices only belatedly that his knees are getting stiff. As he tries to stand up awkwardly, he nearly falls, photos in hand, just as the body of Franck Terrail fills the doorframe.

What are you up to there? asks the chairman.

10

Franck Terrail's body is large, solidly built, statuesque, and well proportioned. Like Luigi Pannone, Terrail has a mustache, but the two bear no relation: as much as Pannone's is a brief, linear ornament, so Terrail's is luxuriant and impressive, massive and serious; it imposes itself as if its wearer were born for it, conceived to display it from the moment he came into the world.

At once reassuring and majestic, authoritarian and benevolent, Franck Terrail's mustache is not assertoric but apodictic: one doesn't ask oneself why he grew it, one can simply not imagine him without the feature, which he is now smoothing with his fingertips as he ponders Pannone, asking once more what he's up to but in a less assured tone, before collapsing onto a chair with a sob.

Now we've had it, thinks Pannone, watching the shoulders of his boss shrug in convulsive jerks to the rhythm of his weeping, tears streaming from his eyes, while from his nose dribbles a viscous fluid, and these liquids run into his mustache, where they blend, and it's very sad to see, and Chairman Terrail looks no more chairman-like than you or me.

Because of these photos, because of little Louise, Pannone hazards, is it because of them that you . . . ? He doesn't need to finish his sentence, and Terrail nods frantically while producing a kind of muddled whistle. Still, it's not, Pannone tries to reassure himself, some sort of blackmail thing some-body sent you? No, no, Franck Terrail hiccups, I had them taken. And I can't stop looking at them, believe me, I can't. Oh jeez, exclaims Pannone. Afraid so, Terrail acknowledges. There, I've told you everything. But after all, it's Louise, Pannone ventures, you know perfectly well that... Yes, moans Terrail between two spasms, I know. His lachrymal outbursts having calmed for a moment, he now emits a long breath. Sixty-eight, Christ almighty, sixty-nine in April. Not right for someone my age, he sniffles, before breaking down again.

It's very awkward, Pannone synthesizes as the other starts bawling again. Especially since she's Nicole's daughter, I mean, after all, he hesitantly points out, you see. I know, moans Terrail, pulling a rumpled Kleenex from the pocket of his bathrobe. I know perfectly well, you know, he blows forcefully. I know, he whispers again, humidly. Can't help it. Stronger than me.

On top of which, Pannone notes, with what's happening with Nicole right now. What about Nicole? Terrail seems to resurface. Oh, right, true, there's that, of course, it's wor-risome, he recognizes, but with no more gravity than if he were speaking of a leak under the sink. Excuse me, but on that note, Pannone instructs him, we need to go. Go? Go where? Terrail laments. The staff has organized a public meeting, Pannone summarizes. About Nicole. We absolutely have to react, we can't do anything without you. They've found a hall in Pantin at the last minute, everything else was booked. Have to go. Sure, Terrail resolves. If you say so.

Luigi Pannone rapidly cooks two fried eggs, at which Terrail nibbles, then they hit the road and night is about to fall, but the roadster is not very comfortable. Push your seat back, Franck, Pannone advises, since Terrail's high knees, rising past the bottom of the windshield, are blocking his view of the landscape. They organized this a bit helter-skelter, Pannone explains, but it was necessary. We mustn't look too destabilized. We have to react firmly, it's important, the TV will be there and everything. Terrail, meanwhile, laterally and distractedly ponders the facades whizzing by, seems to be interested in the Seine when they cross it, and why didn't you take the beltway instead? Not really the best time of day, Pannone indicates. You know, Franck, he adds in a lower register, you're going to have to say something. I don't know if I can, the chairman shifts around, the better to accommodate his rear end on the bucket seat. I'm unhappy, Luigi, he rants. Ah, I'm terribly unhappy and I hate this.

They have thus crossed Paris southwest by northeast up to Pantin, where the IPF tech support has rented, for want of a better place, a gymnasium. A certain number will attend, especially local militants; the sections have mustered the troops, emotion is the order of the day, the decor is plain, especially since they've had no time to prepare. A hundred or so persons standing before a stage, on which several of the movement's leaders are lined up in plastic chairs, its director general, Joel Chanelle, in the middle, beneath a somewhat used banner on which you can make out the yellow-and-green logo of the Independent Popular Federation. Louise is present in a dark gray tailored suit, not far from Guillaume Flax and Cedric Ballester, both in navy blue, with Dorothée Lopez in back.

They parked where they could, greeted the security staff as they entered the gym. Pannone took Terrail's arm as they passed through the audience and went up to the stage, where Chanelle, still rubicund, plump, and coiffed, was discoursing. Pannone installed Terrail in the chair to the left of the podium, slightly removed from the other seats, then joined Francis Delahouère on the floor. It was a deliberate choice, Chanelle bloviated, to use this modest hall to render homage to our national secretary. This place represents our people and, in so many words, their demand for change. Give me a break, grumbled Delahouère.

Francis Delahouère, personal assistant to Joel Chanelle: spheroidal aspect like the latter's, but in a ragged, imprecise, untidy version. His tie peeks out from his shirt collar, his hair is restive, and his clothes, even when new, appear frayed at the extremities; he looks like a portrait of Chanelle drawn by a psychotic child. He clucks his tongue listening to Chanelle hammer home that they will not respond to this provocation. Any ideas about who's behind it? Pannone inquires in a murmur. Behind what? asks Delahouère. Nicole, Pannone summarizes. No idea, grimaces Delahouère. Words fail me, Chanelle continues all the while, to express our sorrow, our concern, and especially our outrage.

Some in the audience cheer loudly, others boo, which Chanelle quiets with the flat of his hand. An agitated young man in a yellow-and-green T-shirt hollers an obscure utterance toward the stage, a television camera pans toward him, two militants rush forward to pacify him with karate chops. We're not really sure who might have done this, Delahouère continues in a low voice. Little shitheads like that guy over there, the opposition, or maybe just nutjobs. Fanatics from the Mozzigonacci faction, maybe.

Our outrage, Chanelle is meanwhile vociferating into the mic, our rebellion, will not stop protesting against the permissive institutions that are alone responsible, nay, guilty, of paving the way for this odious act. The jeering starts up again, and this time Chanelle does nothing to calm it. He resumes and concludes his speech with an homage to Chairman Terrail, whom we assure of our affection and in whom we reaffirm our complete trust in this trying moment. We are with you, Franck. If you'd like to say a few words. Terrail gets up from his chair more easily than expected.

A minor stir occurs at that moment in the audience. Ah, the little doctor's right on time, remarks Luigi Pannone, and we see that doctor, Jean-François Bardot by name, wending his way through the crowd, while Terrail, rather than babbling, as Pannone had feared, improvises a brief but effective allocution about gathering forces, not giving in to hatred, and persevering.

You gotta hand it to him, Franck's still got it, Delahouère observes as Jean-François Bardot, all smiles, advances on Pannone with hands and teeth forward. So, inquires the doctor, how can we be of use? It's complicated, Delahouère raises his voice as the audience applauds Terrail, we can't trust the police, they're on the other side. The pros don't want to get involved, they want no part of it, which I understand. We'll have to find someone unconnected with all this, Pannone suggests half-heartedly. I don't know, an independent agent of some kind. They gaze at each other, pondering. Together, together forever! Franck Terrail is concluding forcefully under the acclaim. I might have an idea, says Bardot. The others turn to face him.

11

I NEVER saw the old man again, never heard from him, maybe he found his Janine all by himself or maybe he replaced her with some Sylvette or Josiane, he never let me know one way or the other, peace be on his sex drive, on top of which his check bounced. Moreover, I never saw anyone else, except once, two days later, another oldster not quite as old; it didn't go anywhere either but it radically changed things: I'll explain.

Having bought two new Bics as a precaution, a red and a blue, I had no trouble engraving the name of this new client on the slate of my notepad using the blue: Pierre-Yves La Mothe-Marlaux. From the name, the scarf knotted about his neck, the signet ring glimmering on his pinkie, and the crest sewn onto his breast pocket, I inferred the individual's degenerate end-of-lineage. Profession: head of corporation. What sort of corporation? I ventured to ask. Signifying with an anteroposterior wave of his hand that all that was long gone, he answered that he'd been involved, among other things and back in the day, with the National Syndicate of Horse Owners for Harness Racing. I pretended to understand and what brings you here today?

It was another case of a disappearing woman, this one named Roberta. Already envisioning myself specializing in this sort of business, I rubbed my hands together in petto and composed a knowing air. As I proposed that he tell me more, La Mothe-Marlaux suggested that it would be better for us to go to his place, so I could form a clearer idea. It was an opportunity to get some air, I agreed, we walked out onto rue Erlanger and headed toward his car, and on the way he pointed out that that building over there, on the corner of rue d'Auteuil, was the headquarters of the National Syndicate of Horse Owners for Harness Racing. I affected an interested demeanor, we got into his Peugeot, the ride wasn't long.

You can't imagine how chic the homes in this area can be. La Mothe-Marlaux's place was the epitome of nice: spacious one-floor villa, aired out by French windows that opened onto a park—not a garden, a park. Vaguely sloping was this park, with paths intertwining among the flower beds, groves, bowers, a bunch of things like that. Just the shed in back to the left, which no doubt contained horticultural implements, would have amply served as my primary residence, and from the terrace one enjoyed a majestic view of the Seine, beyond which lay Neuilly. La Mothe-Marlaux lingered, watching my eyes. I sensed he was delighted to see me taken in by his holdings; it was getting annoying, and I proposed we go inside. Perhaps you'd like to see Roberta's room, he suggested. Good, I nodded, let's go see her room.

Fine, it was a lady's bedroom, I don't know how else to describe it. Nothing to mention except a large bed, an armoire stuffed with dresses, a settee with side tables of different heights, as well as a writing desk whose drawers I opened: a bunch of household papers that I ignored, a fat bundle of brochures proposing overseas voyages from a travel agency whose address, you never know, I jotted down. With my red ballpoint, to economize on the blue. And because that variation in the noting of clues might give La Mothe-Marlaux, who stuck to me like glue, an advantageous idea of my professionalism.

I ended up noticing, behind the settee, a half-open door through which, perceptive me, I supposed you reached a bathroom. You did reach one, in fact. This, too, was just a bathroom like any other, but one in which a second door, this one shut, led, when I opened it, to a laundry. I went in, it was hard to see, the light switch was nowhere to be found, and a huge silver gymnastics ball was blocking the skylight above a washing machine. I could nonetheless make out, in front of this household appliance, a shape that I approached, pulling from my pocket a slender flashlight—I was prepared, the job was beginning to sink in—before immediately stepping back. And that, I asked without turning around, what's that supposed to be?

That was a person sitting in a chair, torso tied with rope to the chairback, head engulfed in a yellow plastic bag held in place with tape with PROTECT OUR ENVIRONMENT! printed on it. This person seemed, first, to be dead, despite my scant experience in the matter, and second, of the female sex, given the outfit.

I stretched out my hand toward the person's neck, as I had seen done when someone wants to determine whether a person is dead or not. It's an artery, I supposed, that they look for in those cases, I was not sure exactly which artery, and in any case, for lack of training, I knew I wouldn't find it. Artery or no, the person's skin was so cold and almost woody that it spoke eloquently. Then I caught sight of a knife resting on her knees, with a red handle and a blade that was also red, but not the same shade. I picked up the knife by its handle, looked at it, put it back down. All of a sudden I realized I had no idea what to do and this was very disturbing.

Don't you think this is disturbing? I asked, but when I finally turned around, La Mothe-Marlaux wasn't there to answer.

I looked for him in the bathroom in vain; then, when I tried to look elsewhere, I couldn't: the door to the bedroom was now locked. I began to suspect foul play, became agitated to the point that I couldn't think straight. It was only when I realized that I was locked alone in a room with a dead woman and my fingerprints were all over these eight square yards, then heard the approaching whine of a police siren, that I realized just how big of a mess I was in.

Since the bathroom had no window, I rushed back into the laundry. I didn't hesitate to climb onto Roberta's knees— I heard the knife fall—to try to move the gymnastics ball and get to the skylight. As the ball was tightly wedged and resisted my attempts, I had to climb back down and pick up the knife, then climb back onto Roberta to puncture it, before pulling it away and opening the skylight, through which I labored to extricate myself, which, given my format, was no mean feat. I fell behind the house from not too high up. I remember there was a barbecue under a cover and some empty flowerpots on a bed of clinkers. I also remember running but not which path I took, I don't recall too well how I managed to regain rue Erlanger but I remember perfectly the moment when, once back home, I decided to change professions.

A week went by, during which I hung fire. I violently felt my mediocrity at having let myself be caught in a trap like a novice, which, moreover, I was, and I didn't want to remain one. I filed for the bankruptcy of FAB and ripped off the Dymo tape, after which I put the maternal armchairs back in their place and restored my waiting room for personal use.

At the end of that week, given the state I was in, I thought about going back to see the psychiatrist; it couldn't hurt to talk things over and get out of the neighborhood. I decided to go on foot, passing by the Michel-Ange–Molitor metro stop, near whose entrance sat a newsstand, where, as I glanced over the headlines, I saw that they were less about the Auteuil disaster: the kidnapping of the Tourneur woman had stolen much of its territory on the front pages.

I approached the Seine, then followed it for about four miles, against the current, in no hurry. It wasn't warm out but I took my time looking at the tethered barges along the quayside with decks full of potted plants, garden furniture, and padlocked bicycles; the tugboats laden with sand, coal, and gravel; the pleasure craft and private yachts; the self-propelled tourist boats and the scows flying Belgian flags; the inflatable dinghies of the river patrol on whose tubes, masked and webbed in black, divers sitting opposite each other waited patiently, immobile and arched like scale models, and I arrived at rue du Louvre.

Heading toward the medical center, I avoided raising my eyes to the opposite side of the street so as not to meet the mocking and perhaps pitying gaze of Duluc Detective. At the reception, they confirmed that my doctor was in, asked me to wait a moment; when I entered his office on the second floor, he was talking on the phone but gestured for me to have a seat. You tell him it's urgent, he emphasized, Dr. Bardot says so, then he hung up, gave me an uncharacteristic look while adjusting his tie, which, as always, matched his pocket square and socks on a background of British twill. Well, Mr. Fulmard, he said in a more cheerful tone than usual, how are we today?

I told him the whole story—my attempt at reemployment, the founding, then the failure of the Fulmard Assistance

Bureau—without saying a word, of course, about the La Mothe-Marlaux incident. It seemed to interest him, even when I said I was giving it up; I hadn't expected that reaction, so I continued. It was an understandable failure, since I was just a beginner, I pathetically admitted. That said, I also claimed, I learned things that should help me find a job. I didn't believe a word of it. He sat up behind his desk, still gazing at me with that uncharacteristic look in his eyes. As for me, at that moment I was staring at my shoes. I might have an idea, said Bardot. I turned to face him.

12

AND THAT'S how I entered into their service.

Note, the idea that Bardot claimed to have, he didn't explain it to me right away, didn't even give me time to react: he got up from his desk, grabbed his raincoat, and motioned for me to follow. We went to the ground floor of the therapeutic institute, reached its five-car parking lot, and with a jerk of his head he indicated his Audi. We got in and he pulled on a pair of driving gloves, grinned at his dentures in the rearview mirror, slid on beige Vuarnets, tuned the radio to Radio France Internationale—while I struggled with the seat belt, unable to fit the tongue into the buckle. We headed off without his saying a word about his plan. We drove toward the southwestern part of the city in a silence filled only by RFI, which gave a brief update on the kidnapping of Madame Tourneur—the trail, they said, was growing cold—then Bardot raised a finger and an eyebrow and glanced briefly at me without a word, nothing more. We arrived in the fifteenth arrondissement, near Boucicaut.

The psychiatrist parked his car in front of a '70s-era building at the back of an alley: executives' cars and executives' wives' minicars with some surrounding greenery, awnings with faded stripes over plate glass windows, entrances tiled in marble with dubious grouting. He signaled that this was the place, I'd expected better, the elevator was slow.

On the fifth floor, to the left, Bardot rang. A blond thirtysomething opened and asked us to wait a moment in the foyer, where rolled-up posters and tied-up bundles of broadsides lay scattered about, and on one wall was an announcement of candidacy with a black-and-white photo, apparently historic, as it was framed under glass. To pass the time, I read the caption underneath, which specified in Gothic script: FRANCK TERRAIL'S FIRST CAMPAIGN FOR DEPUTY OF THE TERRITOIRE DE BELFORT IN THE LEGISLATIVE ELECTIONS OF 1978, FOR THE DEMOCRATIC MOVEMENT PARTY. The blond came back for us and we entered a very austere parlor where we found, seated at a table, a man and a woman whose names Bardot didn't mention.

I was the one he introduced to them, and even then only barely: just a jerk of the jaw toward my person, as if he were noting the delivery of an object, which irritated me. Have a seat, Gerard, he nonetheless offered. He had never called me by my forename, and we might suppose that doing so now would have made me less irritated, but no. The man at the table looked at me devoid of expression or anything else, again as if I were a delivered object, then he turned to the woman and seemed to assent. Not a word for a long moment, it was becoming oppressive until the woman broke the ice by offering me some coffee. As I murmured just a glass of water, she signaled to the blond, who disappeared, no doubt toward the kitchen. Finally she smiled at me: I am Attorney Dorothée Lopez, she stated.

Attorney Lopez incarnated the type of slightly mature woman that one must come across in the types of social gatherings of which I had only a vague idea, and who—champagne flute in hand, smoky voice and smoke-gray tights, abyssal décolleté and extraterritorial red lipstick—negligently lets a strap of her dress slip while quoting Plekhanov on the tip of her fat pink tongue, and the mechanism works every time: I have to look away or I'll get a stiffy. When she also began spontaneously calling me Gerard, I felt a blush rising and choked on the glass of Contrex that the blond, bottle in hand, had just handed me.

Gerard, she said, let me introduce Cedric Ballester. Said Ballester nodded. Although seated, said Ballester seemed rather tall, with a fashion model's physique, petrol-blue suit and tie, brown hair like steel wool. He managed a frozen half smile. We're going to need your help, Attorney Lopez went on, as our friend Bardot has no doubt explained. I didn't go into any detail, stated Bardot, who, hands behind his back, stared at the bare walls as if they weren't. It's a somewhat delicate matter, she specified, a small surveillance job. Jean-François has told us it's your specialty. Guillaume will indicate what procedures to follow.

So the blond's name was Guillaume, and I weakly tried to object that I wasn't very qualified—all the while hinting that it remained to be seen, for jobs don't come along every day. Attorney Lopez blinked tenderly and pouted her lips while emitting a *tut-tut* with her fat pink tongue against her teeth, no doubt to evaporate my vague scruples, then she turned toward the aforementioned Cedric Ballester and everyone began talking as if I didn't exist.

Cedric Ballester uttered some technical statements that flew over my head, the others ratified them blindly, then they all debated at once. They referred often to a certain Franck—not without resigned admiration—who I soon realized was the politician Terrail, whose old campaign poster hung in the foyer. Attorney Lopez occasionally turned toward me with a pacifying smile, no doubt to reassure me about the continuation of my biological existence. As for Ballester, I seemed to gather that he was something like Terrail's spiritual son. They agreed with him constantly and respectfully. Yes, Cedric. Of course, Cedric. Absolutely, Cedric. Meanwhile, I was still unclear about what it was they wanted from me.

After a moment, at a sign from Attorney Lopez, the blond approached me. He had the pleasant face of an underling or estate manager at whose home one organizes this type of meeting, rather than at the leader's house or party headquarters. He introduced himself: Guillaume Flax. He showed me a Post-it with *Guillaume Flax* written on it, followed by a telephone number—just in case, he soberly informed me—then he pulled from his pocket an envelope onto which he stuck the Post-it, before handing them to me.

That done, Bardot took me aside and said: Okay, Fulmard, I imagine you're very busy, we won't keep you any longer. This time, he used neither Mr. nor Gerard; he called me by my surname in order to gently kick me out and let me return home by metro. I left without further ado, with a vague goodbye and via the stairs.

On the ground floor, two men were waiting for the elevator. A short, nervous, dark type escorting a huge, glum more-than-sexagenarian. I supposed they were going to join the others on the fifth floor, since I recognized the huge, glum one as Franck Terrail, whom I'd seen on television—though less often than his accomplice, Chanelle—and just recently, in a younger incarnation, on his poster. Terrail had changed a lot since the Belfort campaign. His tired eyes, hovering above their bags as if ready to sink into them for a snooze, rested slowly on things and stuck there, then tore themselves away, painstakingly changing direction to go cling to something else: a viscous gaze that, in any case, ignored me. The elevator arrived, they got in, I went out.

Squeezed into the elevator cabin, Luigi Pannone gives Franck Terrail a prop master's final once-over before the latter goes onstage. Noting sadly that, the bottom of his shirt having come undone, Terrail's tie dangles over a triangle of nude, hairy, hemispheric belly: Your buttons, Franck, Pannone signals in a whisper. Then, on the fifth floor, Flax opens the door.

In the apartment, everyone stands upon their entrance. Ballester leaves ajar a servile smile, Bardot puts down a magazine, and Dorothée Lopez slips two strands of hair back into place while Terrail sits down and closes his eyes. Where do things stand? Pannone asks in his stead. Because Franck is pretty worried, you know? We've found someone, declares Lopez, one of Jean-François's patients. What kind of someone? Pannone inquires.

13

On the metro that brought me back from Boucicaut to Michel-Ange–Molitor, and even more so during the transfer at La Motte-Picquet–Grenelle, where there is always a decent-sized crowd, I pressed the envelope in my inner pocket tightly against my breast. I hadn't dared check it immediately, reassuring myself by constant fingering that it hadn't moved, and didn't open it until I was back on rue Erlanger: it contained money and papers.

First, the money. I counted three thousand euros in bills of one hundred. This total delighted me, its distribution a bit less, as I'm not a devotee of large denominations. And since, given the current absence of a hypermarket, I shop in a minimart on rue d'Auteuil whose manager rightly assumes me to be economically enfeebled, I imagined his suspicious manner on taking one of these bills between reluctant thumb and index and casting an incredulous eye on it before passing it through his counterfeit detector.

Next, the papers consisted of identification records: names, addresses, photographs of two individuals whom, if I had understood Attorney Lopez correctly, I was supposed to watch. I read the first record: Mozzigonacci, Jean-Loup; the name didn't ring any bells, nor did the photo. But the second photo made my breath stop short, my heart skip a beat, and my eyes widen without needing to read the name: Tourneur, Louise.

I believe I've mentioned my liking for this young woman, even without having ever seen her in the flesh. I was moved, the sheet trembled at the tips of my fingers. I could have delayed my pleasure and handled this Mozzigonacci first, but, not being one to save the best for last, I decided to start with Louise Tourneur. And pronto.

On the back of the record, Flax had drawn a cursory map of her place of residence, apparently difficult to access. An X marked what must have been the service entrance to a residential building, and above that X was a long, complicated entry code. I memorized the map, learned the code by heart, and equipped myself—supple shoes, anorak with multiple pockets, binoculars—then went back into the metro to head for the place, somewhere between La Muette and Sablons.

While the ride was not long, my recon of the building in question, on the other hand, was time-consuming, so well was it camouflaged; but after circling it three times, I finally discovered the service entrance, and the code worked.

I immediately spotted two watchmen on their rounds, which edified me as to the level of security. When they had disappeared, I had little difficulty locating Louise Tourneur's villa, which was clearly indicated on the map; I noticed an adjacent swimming pool bordered by a row of agaves and posted myself behind one of them. As this ornamental plant was roughly of my height and width, its placement seemed ideal: without being seen from the villa, I could enjoy a good panorama from among its thick leaves, and I began to wait.

I waited, it was very quiet, very calm: breath of the filter pump in the pool house, growl of a Lamborghini Aventador V12 engine along a drive path, cheeps of swifts and blackbirds, I waited a long time.

Such a long time, without anything happening, that I began doubting the relevance of my presence, got bored, so to kill time I studied my agave more closely. Back when I was unemployed, I'd read in a book that agaves were used by the ancients for all sorts of things. From their teeth they made nails, styluses, hairpins, needles, and toothpicks; from their stalks they fashioned flutes; and, after turning the leaves into fiber, they knitted clothes, ropes, and hammocks. From the agave one could also extract medicines to treat arthritis and constipation, but also excellent liqueurs and perfectly respectable shaving cream, not to mention that their spine correlatively functioned as a razor. In short, everything was useful about the agave, which in addition was serving me at present as a hideout, perhaps pointlessly, it was indeed a long time.

From waiting in a more or less squatting position, I was beset by all sorts of pins and needles, pricklings, numbings, and other disagreeable paresthesias, but after forty-five minutes I was pleased not to have sat there for nothing. When Louise Tourneur finally appeared, in a half-open beach robe and unlaced sneakers, a bath towel slung over one shoulder, I grabbed my binoculars. The latter were not very new or of particularly high definition, but were good enough to let me see the labels BALENCIAGA on the shoes, GUCCI on the robe, as well as much more interesting things once the latter had dropped.

Louise Tourneur: I don't understand those who critique certain peculiarities of her anatomy, supposedly her chin, her strabismus, and her feet. On the contrary, those details attract me even more: her willful jaw, the slight indecisiveness of her gaze that makes her seem enigmatic and hazy, her larger-than-average extremities, as I could ascertain when she removed her sneakers.

Instead of diving straight in, as I'd anticipated, she climbed down the ladder, her size 10s followed by her calves and thighs, but reluctantly, as if confronting water that was colder than anticipated. Then, as she abruptly submerged her waist, Louise Tourneur let out a brief sigh of fear, surprise, delight, as if encircled by an unexpected limb rather than by a swimming pool—which moved me even more than Attorney Lopez had that same morning—before launching into a perfect crawl. I fixed my binoculars on her 120 backs-and-forths, again the wait was long but better than before.

When she emerged from the water, I stared even harder as she wrapped herself in her towel. It was then that a young man with tawny complexion came running toward her, holding out an electronic tablet. Louise Tourneur seized the appliance, looked at the screen; it must have been serious and it happened quickly: I saw her face fall and grow pale, she tried to speak but must have felt faint, for, suddenly losing her balance, she fell back into the water, where she began making incoherent movements as if, all at once, she'd forgotten how to swim.

The young man immediately dove in to help her, but he must have done it poorly, as the surface of the pool began to bubble: from where I was, I saw arms and legs tangling to no effect. As they wriggled about and haphazardly grabbed at each other without result, I could easily imagine the two of them drowning, and I don't know what came over me, but, throwing caution to the wind, I rushed toward the basin to try to come to their rescue, and then things did not go at all as planned.

I must have gone about it rather poorly myself; in any case, I didn't choose my angle very well. A characteristic of the agave that I've neglected to mention is its aggressiveness, given its barbed stalks that end in sharp points. I got entangled in them, was lacerated in various places, and fell heavily, immediately attracting the attention of a second young man, whom I hadn't seen, just as tawny of complexion but also flanked by a giant black schnauzer, who rushed toward me while exhorting said animal. Restrained by a leash, just barely, the canine rose on its hind legs, not letting me out of the sight of its bloodshot eyes, chops wide open and drooling and growling dully while the tawny young man shouted at me not to move. Fine, I said, fine, it's all good. Just hold on to that dog.

14

IT'S LIKE she's asleep, Terrail murmurs, don't you think?

Luigi Pannone touches the PAUSE icon on his tablet and, on-screen, Nicole Tourneur indeed seems to be fast asleep except that she's dead. Dressed in the random way that people tend to clothe hostages—sweatsuit top on which you can make out the crest of FC Bayern Munich, and mismatched jogging pants—she is framed at mid-thigh in medium close-up, lying on a kind of bed frame made of plastic or metal or painted wood, it's hard to tell which, while behind her rises a tan wall and that's it.

Pannone touches START but it doesn't change anything, since Nicole Tourneur is motionless; he turns up the volume to maximum but it's only a phantom of sound, the ambient mic not having been muted: something like a noise can be made out but it's only a continuous whisper, gray and muffled, a pure, flat, mechanical breath. They filmed the lifeless body without commentary, evidently thinking it would suffice, as they appended no manifesto, no demands, zero communiqué.

It must have been lunatics who did this, judges Terrail. I'd say more like amateurs, nuances Pannone; if I were them, I'd have removed the Bayern crest. On a notebook pulled from his pocket, he jots down a few facts. The twelve-second video was sent without comment via cybernetic means to

Franck Terrail's domicile—as well as to the home of his stepdaughter, Louise Tourneur—at 4:24 p.m. It is now 5:06. Pannone notes all this while Terrail stands up and goes to stare at the landscape, from the high reaches of his skyscraper.

At his feet, in the foreground, delimited vertically by the iron-gray ribbon of the Pont de Bir-Hakeim and the bister-and-white ribbon of the Pont de Grenelle, and horizontally by the cordons of quays fringed with beige corniced buildings and edifices braided with red-tinged deciduous trees, the brown scarf of the Seine runs motionlessly, divided into two sections by the gray plait of the Île aux Cygnes, onto which Nelson Towers and its neighbors cast long rectangles of shadow.

Beyond this frame, the urban prospect looks like a huge, sloppily made bed buried under a hodgepodge of fabrics, stone shawls and concrete lap rugs, mufflers of building stories and ruffles of balconies, terrace coverlets over the rumpled monochrome of light-colored sheets, a patchwork of pale bedspreads with squares of zinc, lead, slate—and farther on, at the horizon's edge, the city turns harborlike onto a hazy sea of extended suburbs, their boundaries marked by the fortress of the Hyatt Regency Hotel standing in as a lighthouse.

It's actually pretty nice, but Franck Terrail sees nothing, his gaze spins in the void, barely does he hear Pannone's voice tentatively rising behind him. Did you say something? Terrail asks, turning around after a delay. Yes, says Pannone, I don't want to be insensitive but there are two things to consider. Okay, says Terrail, talk.

The first, Pannone ventures, is that this changes everything. You no longer have anything to blame yourself for, I mean about little Louise. No, but, Luigi, Terrail reacts, do you hear yourself? Perfectly, intones Pannone. Nicole is dead, it's awful but she's dead and we have to face facts. Your feelings have become ordinary. Silence. All right, Terrail articulates soberly, and the second? But at that moment someone buzzes at the door, Pannone goes to answer, Dorothée Lopez appears.

Lopez has changed since the last time they saw her. The tragic circumstances and their no doubt contentious repercussions have caused her to adopt an outfit halfway between bereavement and combat: strict charcoal-gray suit accessorized with a camouflage-pattern silk scarf, Doc Martens with laces and topstitching on air-cushioned outsoles. She pulls from her handbag a cell phone, which she brandishes in front of Franck Terrail's eyes. Ah, sighs Terrail, you got the video too? You're joking, Franck, Lopez supposes, everyone got it. They're showing it in a continuous loop on every channel, social media, all of it. Ah, exhales Terrail.

Let's get back, Luigi Pannone cuts in, to that second thing. What was the first? asks Lopez, but they don't answer. I'm talking about succession, Pannone continues. The national secretary has left us, it's unfortunate but that's how it is. The thing is, now we need a replacement, and fast.

With that, the debate over succession is underway. Names are invoked: Chanelle, Delahouère, Ballester, and even Franck Terrail himself. No, says Terrail, I'm too old. Too tired. Arguments confront each other, the specter of Mozzigonacci briefly hangs in the air—one always has to factor in Mozzigonacci—latent antipathies surface, reunifications are envisioned, proposal follows proposal, they get nowhere.

They get a bit further when Pannone explains that in this moment of crisis, it would be better to have a woman lead the general secretariat, even if they have to reconsider later.

Dorothée Lopez starts to blush and squirm, but no, Pannone immediately disillusions her, frankly, I can only imagine Louise to ensure the transition. A mother replaced by her daughter, he stresses—seems clear to me it would be perfect. Louise won't accept, Terrail objects. Succeed Nicole—she'd never agree. And she has no experience. She won't agree at first, Pannone snickers, but you know how women are, you know how people are in general. And as for experience, that's what *we're* here for. Not to mention, Franck, he winks, it could be good for you. Silence. What do you mean by that, Luigi? asks Lopez. Nothing, says Pannone.

They debate a moment longer, with decreasing conviction, then end up agreeing on the Louise solution. In that case, Franck, Pannone concludes, you have to talk to her. She has to be convinced and you're the decisive voice. The moral authority of the party, I can't imagine anyone else. Fine, Terrail exhales again. Another silence. I think I'll be going, declares Dorothée Lopez, standing up, I have things to do in court. Dorothée, Pannone calls after her, not a word of this to anyone, you got it? Come on, Lopez smiles, of course.

15

DOROTHÉE Lopez takes the elevator. It's too big for her alone, that elevator, too many mirrors for her self-esteem, and, especially, way too fast, so much so that during the descent she feels something like a lurch rising like a counter-current in her internal organs, a vague vertical wave running through her from pubis to larynx: not great. Once she's outside Nelson Towers and mechanically raises her eyes, the summit of the tall building crowned with clouds, this time in worm's-eye view, causes her to feel a violent vertigo. Really not great either, and Dorothée Lopez resents these malaises that she never reveals to anyone, that no one would ever suspect in someone apparently so sure of herself, so authoritarian and ruthless. But not in the slightest: Lopez is much more emotional than she lets on, more fragile, more fanciful, she envies those clouds for not being prone to vertigo, although when you get down to it, what do I know.

She hails a passing taxi, climbs in, gives the address not of the law courts but of a golf course in Rueil-Malmaison, and the driver sets off. Now, from the Front de Seine to Rueil-Malmaison is a rather long and dreary route, a repetitive and not very interesting landscape: there is little to see that hasn't been depicted a thousand times, nothing to hope for in that regard. So since we have some time on our hands, let's instead use it to sketch out a brief biography of Dorothée Lopez.

The only child of Dr. Patrick Lopez (gastroenterologist in Sèvres, clientele with affluent innards, dean of the Academy of Medicine, recipient of the Shanti Swarup Bhatnagar Prize) and Geneviève Lopez née du Glavial (president of the Federation of Ecumenical Family Councils), young Dorothée stood out through her precociously fierce independence of mind. Quickly terminating her studies after six weeks at the École du Louvre as an independent auditor, she opted for stardom as a career, a fate that nonetheless doesn't happen just like that. She first appeared in a few advertisements—for Moulinex, Ultrabrite, Lactel—then managed to scrape up some walk-ons in alternative-cinema circles before landing a real part, finally, in a real TV movie, her portion of dialogue alas being reduced after editing to these words: "Oh really? Two months?"

Her artistic commitment then frayed, yielding to an accelerated consumption of younger and not-so-young men, each endowed with a very short lay expectancy while she looked for better, this better being a love with a longer shelf life, whom she would follow to the Balearic Islands. We know little about this period of her life, which was interrupted by Dorothée Lopez's hasty return to France, more precisely to a notary's office in Marnes-la-Coquette after the accidental death of Patrick and Geneviève Lopez in the midair explosion of a Fokker F-100 between Brussels and Oslo.

Enough of a dissipated youth, then, to justify the existence of a document discovered at the back of a drawer while emptying her father's desk several days after the crash, which consisted of a card bearing the forename Dorothée, followed by the notation *Don't forget to disinherit her.* Renounced a hundred times by her family, she was, as the nonobservance of this memento attests, a hundred times absolved, unless Dr. Lopez was simply caught short before realizing his plan. Whatever the case, as sole heir of the profits from the upper crust's intestines, Dorothée Lopez found herself rich.

From then on, she could have chosen to do nothing and rest on her gold, but she was restless and, dreading boredom, bravely enrolled in law school. It wouldn't last long, just long enough to acquire sufficient notion to call herself an attorney, whereas she spent her time mostly going out in society, and one fine evening seduced Franck Terrail. That wouldn't last either, Terrail would soon forget that adventure when he met Nicole Tourneur, but, continuing to deploy her charms, Attorney Lopez, Esq., was able to scrounge a place for herself as an image consultant in the org chart of the IPF. She thus became an intimate not only of the Terrail-Tourneur couple but also of their entourage, including several young hopefuls in the party who are champing at the bit. Lopez has slept with one or another of them on occasion, you never know, that's where things stand.

Provisional end of this brief biography that has taken us a half hour without too many stops; in other words, the time needed to travel the eleven miles separating Nelson Towers from the golf course in Rueil-Malmaison, at the entrance to which the taxi lets off Dorothée Lopez.

But she has not come here today to indulge in this sport, even though she began playing it after her return from the islands, once she had the means. Skirting the path that leads to the teeing ground, she heads with a martial step toward the clubhouse, before which golf carts are stationed. She enters: deep armchairs and padded sofas, bar with swivel stools, picture window looking out on a close-cropped green, huge fireplace emblazoned by a panoply of irons, putters, and woods. Dorothée Lopez notices, then joins, Cedric Ballester and Guillaume Flax, slumped around a coffee table near the fireplace, each with an iPad on his knees, each in a golfing outfit: Ballester in a red Altman polo shirt with black stripes and a white collar, mauve Aldrich golf trousers, and a pale blue Rosi pullover thrown over his shoulders, Flax entirely in Decathlon.

Chanelle isn't here? asks Lopez. He's coming, indicates Flax, we're expecting him any minute. I was on the phone with him earlier, says Ballester, he seemed to be vibrating with excitement, he must think his time has come. So we'll have to put him off while leaving him some room for hope, Lopez thinks aloud. It will be delicate. What are you talking about, Dorothée? worries Ballester. Has Franck made a decision? I'll tell all, Lopez announces.

16

ANOTHER brief biography, this time of Moshe Brand, totally mute until the age of five, so much so that his family and the medical authorities they consult deem him mentally irredeemable. No way to get a word out of him until the day when, suddenly, he begins to sing, incessantly, while demonstrating a vocal power, a tonal accuracy, a warmth, and a range such that he plunges the entire kibbutz into stupefaction. During the seventeen years that follow, he sings relentlessly. At the age of twenty-two, having no intention whatsoever of shutting up, he leaves Israel for Paris, where, understanding only Hebrew, he signs abusive contracts without reading them and has to perform his first tune phonetically: "Let Me Love You," a major and immediate hit.

It's under the name Mike Brant, wearing versicolored belted velvet jackets and frilled satin shirts, that he then goes from tour to tour, gala to gala, Olympia to Olympia. Things work out better and better, he kills it on the hit parade, is acclaimed by masses of supporters, battalions of fans, and megatons of girls who are crazy about him, screaming and bombarding him every night with their jewelry: necklaces, chains, rings, and bracelets pile up at his feet the minute he opens his mouth, until by the end of the concert the stage is carpeted in gold.

This lasts for six years. It goes too fast and it's exhausting.

All those women disappoint him, his producers swindle him, jealous showbiz speaks ill of him, the antidepressants make him fat and compromise his erections, soon he can't stand it anymore and he resolves, at age twenty-eight, on April 25, 1975, at eleven fifteen, to throw himself from a balcony on the seventh floor of no. 6 rue Erlanger, in other words, a few doors down from where I live today.

And from where, that Friday, my mother was just going out to do the shopping at the Auteuil market, such that Mike Brant came this close to landing on top of her. He splattered practically at her feet, she had to go around him, dragging her trolley, then the firemen showed up. Evidently she had no desire to look more closely at the body, certainly she wouldn't have recognized him even if, as one of his faithful fans, long after Mike's death she often hummed in the kitchen the refrain *Who will know, who will know, who will know, who will know how to make me forget, oh tell me so.* This suicide, I was told, became a big deal in the neighborhood, and in all of France, but I wasn't yet born enough to remember it.

Where I live today doesn't look like much, since, having abandoned self-employment, I've resigned myself to restoring the initial layout of my lodgings: no need for a waiting room or office or anything. Still, even while reconstituting the old order, I thought I might improve my habitat a bit, but I constantly hesitated in my initiatives for embellishment—moving things around, only to immediately put them back again; eliminating certain items, only to find a new use for them—and in those conditions, my two and a half rooms no longer knew quite what to hold on to or whom to trust. Let's call it a transitional phase.

Given the injuries resulting from my sequential contact

with the agaves and with Louise Tourneur's Asian gorillas, my body was itself in a transitional phase. The lesions were hidden by my clothes, but I also had a dislocated shoulder and several bruised ribs. Still, I hadn't gotten off too badly with the two tawny men, who, after pushing me around—somewhat roughly, truth be told—then deeming me negligible, had let me go without too much fuss. As for young Miss Tourneur, I don't believe she even saw me.

Considering recent events, I drew up a list and two conclusions stood out. First: each time I'd thought I was onto something, it had quickly gone south. Second: I'd ultimately been lucky, it could have been worse, but at least I'd tried. And, finding myself back at point zero, I thought I might go seek advice from Bardot. Even if he had been my last silent partner and I had failed in executing his instructions, he was above all my therapist; as such, I liked to think he wouldn't hold my failure against me too much. Having decided to consult him, I further resolved to change my outfit so as to make a more favorable impression. But as I started to undress, I observed that one of my socks, the left one, had a hole in the big toe.

Now, what to do in such an eventuality? In such cases, several options and sub-options present themselves. One can throw out both socks, thereby depriving oneself of the one without a hole, which would be a shame. One can also throw out only the torn one—or reuse it as a rag—and conserve the intact one with an eye toward pairing it with another. One then has to wait until another sock in another pair springs a hole, recuperate the intact one, and, via the adjunction of the original intact one, reconstitute a pair in working order. It's more economical but it's no less uncertain: it presupposes that the state of wear of the two intact socks is analogous and at the same time that they are of the same length, color, and material—cotton, wool, lisle, silk, cashmere, or linen—all this by way of hypothesis, for, personally, in summer and winter, I stick to viscose.

I was at that point in my analyses when someone unpleasantly pounded on my door. I jumped, then sped up the procedure, throwing on my clothes at the idea that it could be a new client, that with this one everything might fall into place, that it might finally be the chance of a lifetime, that I'd change later, and I no longer felt my shoulder or my ribs as I ran to the door and opened it.

But I immediately recognized the visitor: Lucien D'Ortho, son of my deceased landlord, Robert D'Ortho, recent victim of Soviet technology. Austere expression on this Lucien D'Ortho, closed face, not a hint of a smile, still in mourning clothes since the disaster, unless he dressed that way in perpetuity. If he looked a fair amount like his father, he especially looked like someone who'd come to demand the rent. My ribs and shoulder made their presence felt again.

17

ON THE morning of the sixteenth, the following events take place, once more around Louise Tourneur's swimming pool. Not far from the basin, on their *goban*, the Nguyen brothers are studying the match referred to as "the blood-vomiting game," which pitted Honinbo Jowa against Akaboshi Intetsu from the thirteenth to the twenty-first of August 1835, Akaboshi playing black.

The sky is overcast, the air chilly, but not chilly enough—any more than the announcement of her mother's death is upsetting enough—to keep Louise Tourneur from effecting her daily laps, this time protected by a swimsuit. It is not out of the question that the black color of this elegantly asymmetrical swimsuit denotes a discreet mourning, or so one could suppose. One could also better detail the recto of her person, as this morning she is expressing herself exclusively in backstroke.

Louise Tourneur really does swim well, without zigzagging or bobbing about awkwardly or making undue effort, classic faults when one ventures into this style, and without bending her legs or letting her shoulders dip too low. She knows how to orient her driving surfaces and her supports, her arms tow her laterally without straying into the depths, her hands extricate themselves from the water via the thumb, as is appropriate for replunging via the little finger. Her airways are clear, her eyes fixed on the overcast sky, and her head, her body's rudder, remains perfectly still. To all appearances, she's had an excellent instructor.

Now, again eluding the attention of the Nguyen brothers, who are clearly distracted, a man has just appeared in the sector. This time, it is neither Guillaume Flax nor Gerard Fulmard, but rather Cedric Ballester, who has swapped his petrol-blue suit for a beige flannel ensemble over a pinkish plain-weave shirt, not bad but not quite "it," you can see he's trying too hard. As he reaches poolside, Louise, who has recognized him, halts at the end of her lap and raises toward him eyes that she then shields with her hand. It's me, Ballester stupidly announces, sorry to bother you, but it would be good for us to talk.

Once out of the water, the young woman shakes her hair, which emits a multidirectional spray of droplets, then wraps herself in her robe while hearing Ballester reiterate that they have to talk. Sure, why not. But, as they barely know each other, what can they say? Topics are hardly lacking, of course: the crisis in the IPF, Louise's hesitancy at being promoted, Ballester's hope of rising in its ranks, Franck's mood swings, or the eternal Mozzigonacci file—there's certainly plenty to tackle, but it so happens that, whether from embarrassment or timidity, Ballester can't seem to decide where to begin. Having started on the matter in a determined voice, the young man now seems at a loss for words.

Because of this loss, or to help palliate it, Cedric Ballester noisily clears his throat, attracting the attention of the Nguyens, who make a show of standing up to intervene. Louise having halted their momentum with her fingertips, the brothers sit back down, but under an umbrella, as other droplets have just appeared, denser and this time coming from the sky. I'm listening, Louise encourages him, albeit in a hardly more assured voice, which only augments Ballester's confusion. And to add drama to the scene, the light suddenly changes, veering at top speed toward an increasingly dark gray, from pearl to anthracite via iron, while the drops multiply, grow heavier, denser and more compact, the surface of the water begins to speckle accelerando, soon they won't even be able to hear each other.

Under this now driving rain, it takes Louise trying vainly to light a cigarette for them to realize they'd do well to seek shelter. Skirting the pool, whose contents are now approaching ebullition, she heads to the villa, followed by Ballester, beneath what is turning into a serious storm, and, once they're in the vestibule, things move pretty fast. Instead of proceeding into the living room, as Cedric Ballester would have imagined, Louise Tourneur resolutely climbs the stairs, barely turning around to verify that he's following. The door to her bedroom, one flight up, is open, and as soon as they've entered, Louise closes it after them: looks, smiles, embraces, etc., the process engages quicko speedo. Shedding the robe and bereavement swimsuit is then a simple operation; Ballester takes longer with his flannel and his plain-weave, no doubt from emotion, his fingers fumble on the buttons, the belt, the laces, but it all comes out right in the end.

The Nguyens, meanwhile, tweak their reconstruction of the confrontation between Akaboshi and Honinbo. Not even the flashes of lightning and claps of thunder following each other in rapid bursts can disturb their concentration, still less in that the displacement of a piece by Ermosthenes, up to now in a bad position, has just spectacularly reversed the power dynamic: Apollodore protests, Ermosthenes stands firm. There follows a long and bitter debate in which various moves specific to this match are invoked, such as the turtle-back, the elephant's move, the monkey jump, and it could go on forever if the telephone in the vestibule didn't start ringing, barely audible in the tumult. Leaving Apollodore to pout, Ermosthenes heads off to answer it with a victorious stride.

Tourneur residence. Yes, hello, Madame Lopez, he pronounces. I haven't been able to get Louise on her cell, Dorothée Lopez exclaims from far away, I'm calling on the landline to let her know about an emergency. I understand, says Ermosthenes. You have to tell her right away, Apollodore, you understand? I understand, but I'm Ermosthenes, Madame Lopez, rectifies Ermosthenes. Yes, Ermosthenes, Lopez whatevers, you have to tell her that Franck, you know, her step-father—I know, I know, says Ermosthenes—Franck has just left for her place and I'm worried, he's all worked up, he's not himself. Tell Louise to be prepared, it's very urgent. I'll take care of it, Ermosthenes assures her.

Ermosthenes hangs up and goes casually—being used to Lopez's vain excitations—to notify his brother, more qualified for this type of mission. Apollodore climbs the stairs just as limply—being afflicted by his defeat—follows the hallway to Louise's bedroom, knocks gently on the door several times, each time a bit louder, without result, until Louise's voice, in a drawling tone, asks what is it. Madame Lopez just called, Madame, Apollodore shouts through the door, to say Mr. Franck is on his way here, Madame Lopez asked me to alert you. He's coming here, Mr. Franck is coming.

18

ON THE afternoon of the sixteenth, then, I showed up at Bardot's. I wasn't there just for him to treat my mental state, but also, given my hematomas, my physical state. I was also hoping he would do something about my financial state, most of the money handed over by young Flax having gone to feed Ortho, Jr., as well as about my future in the ranks of the IPF, after the failure of my mission at Louise Tourneur's. That was a lot, and the time seemed right for a comprehensive reassessment.

In the waiting room of the medical center on rue du Louvre, I leafed through some newspapers. They now barely mentioned the tragic fate of Nicole Tourneur, while the emotion caused by the Auteuil disaster seemed to have totally expired. After the receptionist loudly called my name, I entered Bardot's office but he didn't look up. Dressed that day in a dark green suit enlivened by a pale yellow pocket square, he laboriously shuffled some papers in pastel-colored folders. I sat, waited, Bardot didn't stop fiddling with his files, as if I weren't there. To pass the time, I looked at the decorations on the walls: on one shelf was a throned statuette of vaguely Aztec character, the kind you might find in the duty-free shops of South American airports, flanked by two posters of abstract paintings from German museums.

As the silence was getting long and heavy, I ended up

breaking the ice. Bardot showed not the slightest reaction when, after clearing my throat, I summarized my visit to Miss Tourneur's. I admitted my clumsiness, pleaded inexperience, and offered my apologies for the fiasco. As Bardot still didn't lift an eye from his papers, I moved on to my physical condition, mentioning in a half murmur my damaged ribs and shoulder. I imagined I'd thereby solicit a bit of his attention, a diagnosis, maybe a prescription. Even if his field was the mind rather than the body, he must have studied medicine, must know a little about basic anatomy, but no, still nothing.

I was starting to get plenty annoyed when he finally put away his folders, stood up, then walked to the window, lingering to gaze at who knows what outside, silently and with his back to me. I stopped talking and was about to leave when he turned around: Tell me, Fulmard, he said, before you go we should perhaps talk about you paying back the honorarium we gave you.

I acquiesced with a gulp. As he was finally looking at me, I saw disdain in his eyes, almost repugnance, and it shocked me. That someone should reproach me for having failed was understandable, I'd expected it, but to look as if he considered me beneath contempt made me feel humiliated, and that I couldn't abide.

I don't know what came over me. I bolted out of my seat, skirted the desk, and gripped Bardot by wherever, I didn't take the time to choose, my hand landed on his vest pocket, from which his little pale yellow thing went flying. See here, Fulmard, he yelped, control yourself, for God's sake, but to no avail as I then started to beat him silly. Without method, certainly, but with gusto. It's not my way and I was hardly having an easy time of it, for even as I was hitting him, I was aware that this was counterproductive, that I would be in the wrong no matter what, not to mention that this exercise, given the condition of my shoulder and ribs, hurt me almost as much as it hurt him—but, too bad, I pummeled.

And then something unexpected happened: after three or four punches—to the stomach, the jaw, the testicles, I'm not sure where else—it began to look as if this activity didn't displease him. No longer resisting, not fighting or even trying to protect himself, Bardot began offering his entire physical surface spontaneously and eagerly to my blows. Since at first that seemed absurd, I had to thump him two or three more times to verify that he was, indeed, enjoying it. And as I had no interest in his enjoyment, I stopped.

But having in a way gained the upper hand, I took advantage more than I would have expected, and, pulling a full role reversal, I crudely demanded money. I began to get used to the role of brute, was developing a taste for it, was amazed to the point of no longer recognizing myself—and he, too, seemed almost happy with his own transformation, and, like me, amazed by it: he opened a drawer in his desk, and I noticed how full that drawer was. Since Bardot appeared to be putting that fullness at my disposal, I helped myself abundantly. I was about to close the drawer when he stopped me and suggested I take more, I hesitated, he insisted—Go on, it will make me happy—I didn't want to upset him, so I went for it.

When we sat back down, Bardot seemed much more relaxed. It was my turn to start shaking, as if I'd just made a huge effort or was afraid of myself, violence not being in my makeup. But all in all, I hadn't done wrong, for he started talking to me in calm, measured tones, as one does to a boon companion. He even offered me a drink, went off to find a bottle and two glasses, and I insisted on pouring, serving him first and very meticulously, in a highly stylized manner; it reminded me of my days as an attendant in business class on Boeings. It was only when he raised his glass that I noticed the state of his hangnails, gnawed well beyond fitness for consumption.

As if it were my concern, Bardot then explained the situation within the Independent Popular Federation. As might be expected after Nicole Tourneur's demise, the vacancy in its leadership was sowing disorder, whetting greed, and stoking rivalries. A meeting was scheduled for the day after tomorrow in Caen, at which the candidates would have their say, and it was there, perhaps, that the party's future would be decided. Since the core militants were bitterly split among the applicants, incidents could occur, a firm maintenance of order was advisable, things could get rather tense. Then, suspending this line of discussion and redonning his medical functions, he said: So now tell me, physically, what's wrong?

I again exposed the state of my injured organs, which at his request I then unveiled and he examined. Given what had just happened—my punches, his reaction, the money, and all that—I was a bit hesitant about his palpations, but Bardot mostly behaved himself. He took my blood pressure, had me stick out my tongue, auscultated, took out his prescription pad, and wrote me a script for an analgesic, my own mother couldn't have done better. After that, his gaze became hazy for an instant, as if he were mulling something over, I think he was mulling something over. In any case, something seemed to have happened between us, at least from his viewpoint, for he suddenly peered into my face, not without apparent depth or tenderness, and then said: Listen, Gerard, again calling me by my forename.

19

IT IS THE night of the sixteenth to the seventeenth at 11:30 p.m., and Franck Terrail is alone, standing in front of the four-story Sexodrome located to the west of Place Pigalle, having been dropped there by taxi. Not too many people left at this hour on boulevard de Clichy. Poorly dressed individuals slowly relocate from one bench to another on the median strip, clusterlets of young folk emerge from a concert or elsewhere, a Berber greengrocer lowers his metal shutter. The emporiums of erotic materials have closed, their windows continuing to highlight abundantly perforated lingerie items, aphrodisiac products with diverse modes of administration, pumps with insanely high heels, whips, wigs, life-size dolls, and other accessories that Franck examines with a neutral eye: we cannot make out what's on his mind.

He crosses the boulevard toward the bottom of rue Germain Pilon, at the corner of which stands a young woman, and Franck, you never know, approaches her. Now, this young woman is not at all what he had imagined; moreover, she is not dressed as he imagined. A tout wearing an outfit that borders on severe, she limits herself to distributing flyers extolling the merits of an establishment of nocturnal pleasure named the Somerset, farther up the street. The Somerset is great, she straightaway affirms to Franck, the atmosphere is great, the people are great, and there are really pretty girls, come see. I'm not especially looking for a really pretty girl, declares Franck, I'm looking for a whore.

This blunt formulation is atypical of him, but this evening Franck seems uninhibited. The tout feigns shock, without much conviction: But, sir, prostitution is illegal nowadays, didn't you know that? Come with me instead and check out our place, she suggests, you'll find all you need to have a good time, and the first glass is on the house. Just a quick look. If you insist, Franck condescends. No longer being, this evening, at the point where one more glass will make a difference, he undertakes to climb rue Germain Pilon, hands in the pockets of his raincoat, one of those hands crumpling a yellow-and-green scarf in one of the pockets.

Franck Terrail mounts the street, replaying in his head his visit that morning with Louise: the conversation did not go at all well. Franck had at first come to see Louise, he assured her on arriving, only for a heart-to-heart. To talk about Nicole, the pain he's feeling, his affliction, his dismay, his grief, all that stuff. He had developed the theme, sketching a highly idealized portrait of Nicole, her spirit, her charm, her beauty, her knowledge, and all *that* stuff. Then, lingering on the question of beauty, Franck began comparing Louise to Nicole, highlighting their resemblances, stressing certain features, supposing others, and, when he took her hand, Louise was perfectly happy to go along, but when his hand slid above her elbow, Louise began to stiffen; then, that hand wandering near her shoulder, she claimed she had to check on something and I'll be right back.

Louise obviously didn't come right back, we have every reason to believe she ran straight to Dorothée Lopez's next door. Franck, left alone, waited for a while, then, when this while threatened to become permanent, he more or less understood the failure of his approach, turned in circles for a moment, before admitting to himself that, all things considered, he should probably leave. Exiting the house, as he passed by the pool he snatched a scarf draped over the back of a deck chair, the former, like the latter, striped yellow and green.

Having left Louise's, Franck Terrail chose not to call Luigi Pannone, as he normally would when he felt distraught. He had himself taken by cab toward Place de l'Étoile, while sniffing the scarf. Vaguely informed that it was, or had been, a prostitution sector—we can now make out better what's on his mind—he had the taxi turn for a moment around several arcs of the impeccable circle formed by rues de Presbourg and de Tilsitt, especially at the corners of avenues Hoche and Foch, but he saw no woman suggesting the appropriate profile. He then visited several all-night bars that were open in the afternoon, in that Champs-Élysées neighborhood, but they were almost empty, and in any case devoid of the desired silhouettes. In them he downed various strong liqueurs until early evening, dined on a croque monsieur washed down with another strong liqueur, then, unable to find what he was looking for, but not without a certain single-mindedness, he took another cab that brought him to Pigalle.

At the top of rue Germain Pilon, the Somerset presents an oxblood facade pierced by mirrored windows and a door of shiny reinforced steel. At mid-height, half a dozen scarlet lanterns, one of them askew, hang over vague resin caryatids soiled by pigeons, and above the entrance pink neon depicts a stylized female figure intended to mesmerize the customer. The customer, however, does not enter just like that: he has to ring, wait, then have a bouncer's eye assess him from behind a grilled window before they finally unlock the door.

Once inside, Franck immediately sees that there are a fair number of people in this establishment: guys with girls in microminis at the bar, guys with girls in hyper-décolleté around pedestal tables on which stand magnums of champagne, guys with girls in general. Turned up not too loud, the music wavers between elevator and samba, the lighting is subdued but not as much as all that. Franck doesn't have time to wonder whether he'll sit at the bar or at a table, before a really pretty girl, in keeping with the tout's assertions, heads toward him. She's wearing only a black wasp-waisted corset and garter belt, such as you find in the shops on the boulevard, but a more sophisticated version; she seems completely at ease and so relaxed that you could almost ignore her outfit. Pleasant smile, elegant body language, delicate diction—she could be a student of thermodynamics or constitutional law putting away a little extra cash—the young woman informs Franck without preamble or fuss that it will cost him four hundred euros for a particular service.

Franck deems it a hefty sum but all in all not so much, given the really very pretty girl, he hesitates a bit before accepting the bargain but then notices that one of the fellows in the room is looking insistently his way, and that changes everything. Franck has forgotten that he's sort of famous, that he's a public figure, that people see a picture of him now and then in the papers. Better that they don't see another, much more compromising one in such a setting, in medias res: panicking at the idea that the guy might have identified him, he abruptly turns his back, cuts things short, claims to the girl that he doesn't have enough on him, that he's very sorry but he'll be back.

Without manifesting the slightest offense, the really pretty girl graciously accompanies him to the reinforced door, opens it for him, and, venturing outside—Franck is afraid for an instant that, uncovered as she is, she'll catch cold—tells him about another club, called the Sylvana, on the same street, a bit farther down on the opposite side, specifying tactfully that the girls there are older and not terribly attractive but that it will surely be less costly. Franck thanks her kindly, crosses rue Germain Pilon, and it's ten past midnight.

20

AT TEN past midnight, near Boucicaut, a meeting of IPF executives in an enlarged select committee was about to conclude.

Order of the day: preparation for the meeting in Caen; review of the homage to Nicole Tourneur that will be solemnly delivered on that occasion; drawing up a draft agreement with the Mozzigonacci faction; report by a Belgian correspondent.

Present: Joel Chanelle (executive bureau), Francis Delahouère (general secretariat), Luigi Pannone (security), Guillaume Flax (inter-section coordination), Jacky Bloch-Besnard (Mozzigonacci faction), Simon Van Os (Brussels).

Excused: Franck Terrail, Louise Tourneur, Cedric Ballester, Dorothée Lopez.

While the absence of Franck Terrail (bereavement and health concerns), Louise Tourneur (bereavement), and Dorothée Lopez (logistical preparations in Caen) was unproblematic, that of Cedric Ballester occasioned some debate.

Ballester is neither excused nor detained, Delahouère vehemently stressed, Ballester is absent and that's a whole other story. And I want to know why. I tried calling him all afternoon, Flax indicated, he couldn't be reached. This is unacceptable, hammered Delahouère, I certainly hope he isn't hiding something. Indeed, it's unusual, reckoned Pannone.

I thought he'd been looking a bit tired lately, Chanelle moderated, Cedric has given a lot of himself these last weeks, it might be that. Tired or not, his place tonight was here, Delahouère persisted. Just imagine if we learn someday that he's been fraternizing with the Mozzigonaccis. How dare you, Delahouère, protested Bloch-Besnard. I wasn't talking to you, Jacky, Delahouère lashed out, I'm saying that this absence must be penalized, maybe not a reprimand, but at least a warning.

Calm down, Francis, Chanelle mediated, though I agree it's kind of curious. You should try to find out, my dear Guillaume. Of course, Joel, Flax hastened to oblige, please know that I share your puzzlement.

If the executives had known what occurred earlier that day between Cedric Ballester and Louise Tourneur, they would have wondered a bit less. Given that one must in fact strike while the iron is hot, must never put off until tomorrow what can be done today, indeed that one does not change horses in midstream, we would be justified in supposing that at that instant Cedric was pursuing and elaborating a commerce interrupted that morning by Franck's untimely arrival.

Apart from that controversy, the meeting begun at seven thirty unfolded without incident. They took a break at around nine, had dinner provided by an enterprise specializing in the delivery of prepared foods, Pannone and Flax had a slight disagreement regarding the amount of the tip to bestow on the delivery driver, Delahouère ate more noisily than the others, then they got back to work.

At around eleven thirty, we begin to observe scattered signs of fatigue. Right, Chanelle summarizes, I believe we've examined every point, haven't we? Not about Ballester,

Delahouère reminds him sourly. Fine, Francis, that'll do, Chanelle appeases him, we'll come back to that later. Any questions? No? Then I propose we adjourn.

The meeting ends at fifteen minutes past midnight, time enough for Franck to walk down rue Germain Pilon.

21

At the bottom of that street, the Sylvana Club is a more modest institution than the Somerset, retracted under a narrow, black, blind facade whose upper portion is decorated with five discreet neons: four violet hearts blinking around the orange noun GIRLS. You gain entrance without difficulty or bouncer, you just have to push the door.

Once inside, Franck Terrail finds the atmosphere quite different from that in the Somerset. No ambient music, no special lighting: the neutral half-light of a back court, parlor, or sacristy. The bar is purely pro forma, with neither stools nor drinkers, nor even many bottles in the background, you don't come here for a drink; moreover, almost no one is here. A female sexagenarian with an uninviting face is sitting behind a kind of ticket window, while farther away two other women are sitting next to each other on folding chairs, one a redhead, the other a brunette, and there are two closets in back. Terrail doesn't have time to look over these women—except to note that they correspond fairly closely to what his informer in the wasp-waisted corset had led him to expect—as the redhead immediately stands up and comes to meet him without even asking what he wants, the matter being clearly understood.

To the extent that the light allows one to judge, from up close the woman seems approximately blond rather than red, or else between colorings. With drooping eyelids and nice cheekbones, wide hips and shoulders, she is less attractive and less freshly undergarmented than her sister colleague from the Somerset, indeed more mature but at bottom not as much as all that, nothing that would set you dreaming but nothing prohibitive or truly off-putting. Nor does Franck have time to say anything, the woman indicates without any transition that it will be fifty or a hundred depending on what he wants, and Franck, who doesn't really know, who is no longer certain of anything, tells her that fifty will do it. Minimum bet, as in poker when you're not yet sure of wanting to enter the hand.

This person then guides Franck toward one of the closets, which turns out to be a booth, a sort of alcove isolated by a not very heavy curtain that she draws shut behind them, signaling to her new client to take his place on a sofa without armrests, barely deeper than a car's back seat. Franck sits down, the woman sits beside him, next to the sofa is a shelf supporting a box of Kleenex, a tube of alcohol-based gel, a condom dispenser, and a plush toy. We did say fifty euros, the woman reminds him. Oh, sorry, Franck apologizes while going through his pockets, seeking in vain a bill of that amount, forced to pathetically render exact payment with three tens and a twenty, which the woman jams under the plushie before addressing herself, without further ado, to Franck's pants.

Hoping to personalize the exchange a bit, Franck ventures to ask the woman's name. Angélique, she answers without raising her eyes from her task, and so mechanically that Franck assumes it's obviously a stage name. Expecting her to ask the same question in return, having planned rather ingeniously, it seemed to him, to call himself Gilbert, Franck is disappointed when she abstains.

Angélique, then, proceeds, without hurrying or overly leaning into it, to unbutton the garment, as methodically as would a nurse or a home helper. While she executes this, Franck perceives a dialogue in the neighboring closet, where another woman, in all likelihood the brunette, explains in the English language to her client, no doubt a tourist waylaid by the neighborhood's reputation, what is and is not sexually possible. This brunette, who, for her part, must be named Haydée or Coralie, possesses a prettier voice than Angélique, of a more exciting timbre. Franck wonders whether he wouldn't have done better to end up with her, all the more so in that this Angélique maintains a certain icy distance, Franck even resents her a bit for not seeming to be particularly into what she's doing. Franck is wrong, for Angélique *is* into what she's doing, without ardor, agreed, but she carries out her task, nothing to reproach her for, even if Franck doesn't quite see it that way.

To get into the spirit, as Angélique lingers on a recalcitrant button, Franck respectfully asks if he may touch her breasts. As she doesn't answer, Franck assumes that this is not included in the tariff, refrains from insisting even as Angélique brings his member out into the open, turns to the condom dispenser from which she extracts a unit, tears open its pouch, begins unrolling the latex, and suddenly Franck feels deflated.

Deflated to the extent that there immediately follows an effect of detumescence, and it will be a whole affair, for almost a whole minute, to try to slip the accessory onto Franck's now limp member. This is technically impossible: rubber does not grip onto a flaccid support, it's in the realm of the antinomic. Angélique nonetheless persists against all logic to resolve this aporia until Franck admits that the enterprise is in vain and tells her so, suggesting she let it drop, adding that he's really sorry. Me too, Angélique says politely.

And so everything is over without having begun. While Angélique looks away, Franck straightens his clothes, and, as all this has happened rather quickly and he might still have a little time, he allows himself without much hope to initiate a conversation, asking a few elementary questions such as apart from this what do you do in life. Franck is surprised when Angélique answers, and, in that booth, an ordinary and benign dialogue occurs, the kind sometimes improvised among travelers at a bus stop—except that Angélique professionally addresses Franck with the familiar *tu*, while he, very Old France, sticks to the formal *vous*.

He therefore learns that Angélique, born in the Lot region, practices the profession of server in a brasserie near La Défense, that she is single-parenting her little daughter, works at the Sylvana three nights a week but also plies her trade at home, and on that score, she suggests, she could come someday to his place if he liked. Franck eludes the offer but is touched, takes careful note, begins to feel a liking for this Angélique, who now says: Well, I'll see you out.

She walks him to the door of the club, which she opens for him as had the girl at the Somerset. Franck concludes that this must be standard operating procedure in the trade; then, when he's back out in the street, this Angélique gives him a nice smile, goes so far as to kiss him on the cheek, Franck is moved, Franck is really moved and boldly tries to kiss her nearer her mouth, Angélique ducks away with a pretty laugh and Franck is more and more moved when suddenly the slope of rue Germain Pilon inverts, the whole street starts to spin, Franck just has time to reflect that he feels very tired, that it's been a rough day, and then he falls.

He collapses between two cars, his head flops onto the curb, his superciliary arch is split open. Angélique tries to get him on his feet but the man is heavy, the woman gives up, mentions the police or firemen—No, Franck manages to whisper, especially not the police. Find me a taxi, quick, please, this time finally using the familiar *tu*. Closing his eyes but not losing consciousness, he feels horribly weary but at the same time none of this is so awful, it's not even completely unpleasant, he'd happily lie there to sleep in peace.

Angélique is at a loss. Calling the EMTs or the police could have consequences, complicate her life unduly, in this kind of situation you can count on only anonymous passersby, though at that hour fewer and fewer anonymous passersby frequent rue Germain Pilon. But as luck would have it, here's one who stops, asks what's going on, declares himself a veterinarian, leans over Franck, examines him summarily, and it doesn't seem very serious, this veterinarian diagnoses, his rhythms seem good. It'll pass. He's sturdy, he looks sturdy. I think he's sturdy. Franck thinks not.

22

THE IPF MEETING will be held in the Convention Center in Caen, more specifically in its amphitheater, whose floor, walls, and 539 seats are uniformly carpeted in royal blue.

One might find this capacity feeble for such a manifestation, but one must remember that the Independent Popular Federation is not a major party: enjoying no public funding, it sustains itself essentially on its rounds of dues and thanks to its brigade of volunteers. Without the occasional boost from a Tourneur cousin who struck it rich in mass-market retail, its treasury would sometimes have trouble making ends meet. Moreover, as its affairs are not tracked very assiduously by the media, only two intern technicians from the local France 3 Normandie TV station are on hand, scowling and unenthused, and with whom three pro bonos from the IPF communications unit, complete with rented videocams and mics, try in vain to establish good relations.

Directed by a security contingent overseen by the Nguyen brothers, the militant and sympathizing faction spreads out among the rows, while the members of the executive committee take their seats in the front, leaving them highly visible to the cameras but mainly able to stretch their legs. Before things begin, the audience has plenty of time to admire the gigantic portraits of Franck Terrail and Nicole Tourneur, the latter barred with a diagonal of black crepe, hanging over the rostrum above the emblems of the party arranged in the background.

Reserved for only a dozen or so participants, with neatly lined-up bottles of Cristaline, the platform gradually fills after the public has settled in. Once seated behind their nameplates, the orators adjust their mics, address little signs to such and such comrades in the auditorium, straighten their ties, and riffle through their notes while pouring themselves glugs of water.

Apart from Luigi Pannone, there are the same speakers as at the last meeting in Boucicault, plus Dorothée Lopez. Joel Chanelle displays an expression of contentment; Delahouère, to his right, seems pleased with this contentment. As a possible sign of overture, ideological reorientation, or new balance of power, Jacky Bloch-Besnard, until now the sole representative of the Mozzigonacci faction, and who is in a private conversation with Lopez, today finds himself next to Brandon Labroche. A young, solidly built adherent of the Mozzigonaccian viewpoint, Labroche has resting on his knees a round hat with narrow brim. Arriving last, Cedric Ballester and Louise Tourneur have joined this cohort, taking care to arrive each via a different side of the stage, she left and he right, then not to sit next to each other. Still vacant is the central seat, reserved for Franck Terrail, for whom they now begin to wait.

As they continue to wait, furtive exchanges start up onstage, then intensify. The faces are serious, but the sentiments, behind muted mics, are merely jocular. Delahouère, for instance, asks Flax, who doesn't know the answer, what the after-dinner plans are. Deserting Bloch-Besnard, Dorothée Lopez leans over to recommend to Louise a fitness center on rue Tronchet, while Brandon Labroche approaches Bloch-Besnard sotto voce: Can't you see Old Lady Tourneur engineering her own kidnapping? he insinuates. Shut up, Brandon, an outraged Bloch-Besnard stiffens. It wouldn't be the Terrails' first deception, Labroche slips in with a knowing look. Rumors are going around, I don't know if you're aware. Shut up already, Brandon, bristles Bloch-Besnard, while noting that, as Franck still has not shown up, chatter mixed with waves of impatience is beginning to sprout in the auditorium. Dorothée Lopez, noticing the same phenomenon, stands up to motivate Chanelle, who is beginning to doze off. We'd better get going, Joel, she whispers in his ear, looks like they're getting restless. Chanelle startles awake. But we can't start without Franck. Tough beans for Franck, Lopez hisses, we can't wait any longer. Let's get started, Joel, for God's sake, let's get started.

When Joel Chanelle taps on his mic to indicate that they're getting started, the rumblings settle decrescendo. Once silence is established, the evening begins with the inevitable homage to Nicole Tourneur. Standing erect, chest puffed out, Chanelle recalls her career and her commitments. Her fidelity, her rigor. Her foresight. Her tragic end. Her work left unfinished. A minute of silence.

Under the moral guidance of our chairman, Franck Terrail, who will be here any minute, Chanelle resumes, pointing to the empty center seat, many battles have been waged, often crowned with success. We will unfailingly continue these struggles, in the spirit of our national secretary, to honor her memory. Today we must make a crucial decision: that of her succession. The stakes are essential for the prospects of our movement. Before passing the mic to Cedric Ballester, who embodies the youth and future of our ideas, I'd like to welcome two representatives of the Mozzigonacci tendency. They have agreed to join us on this solemn occasion and I thank them for it. For beyond certain completely secondary differences, we must unite in the name of the shared principles that have always held us together: support for work and a sense of values.

Applause. Chanelle sits down, then turns to Ballester: Your turn, Cedric, over to you. I don't want to speak in Franck's absence, Ballester objects. Over to you, Cedric, we said, Delahouère intervenes. Franck will be here any minute. Go on; otherwise, how will it look?

With no alternative, Ballester stands up and develops the always welcome theme of basic unity. Evoking, while minimizing, the disagreements that might have surfaced with our comrade Jean-Loup Mozzigonacci, he invents the idea that working groups will meet to iron out these minor divergences, which I wish for with all my heart, and all the more fervently in that they are, I am certain, mere misunderstandings. Whatever the result, I like to believe that their conclusions will align with the principles implemented by our late lamented national secretary and defined for many long years by Chairman Terrail. I'm told, moreover, that he will be here any minute, but, before turning over the floor to him, I'd like to underscore our fidelity to these essential principles, which are, first and foremost, a sense of work and support for values.

Applause. Franck, however, is still not there. A lapse follows, and is felt onstage and very soon in the amphitheater, people start giving one another looks. All right, Chanelle murmurs, what do we do now? I haven't got a clue, Delahouère panics, we'll have to wing it. That's right, wing it, Chanelle orders. Wing it, Francis, say something, anything, but be sure to mention my name.

Not having planned to speak, Delahouère has to improvise in turn. He is used to this practice, but, after he's taken the mic and reminded everyone that the stakes of this meeting are decisive, Franck Terrail finally appears at stage right, looking pale and held upright by Luigi Pannone, the bandage above his left eye visible despite the makeup. Did you see how awful he looks, worries Bloch-Besnard. He looks like crap, Labroche amplifies. I said decisive, Delahouère stresses in a higher voice, and I'm choosing my words carefully.

Pannone pulls back the center seat to allow Franck to sit, and that movement at that moment destabilizes Delahouère, who rushes to conclude: Before our chairman takes the podium, I'd like to underscore the weight of our responsibility in establishing the future composition of the national secretariat. It promises to be a daunting task, without a doubt, for whoever ends up succeeding such an irreplaceable figure. But let us have no doubt, in the tradition of our movement, all of us united around our director general will defend the support of work and the value of sense. Chairman, the floor is yours!

Weaker applause. Another pause. Franck decidedly does not look like he's ready to speak. He rummages through his pockets as if to pull out some notes, pulls out nothing at all, then rummages again, pulls out a handkerchief, and loudly blows his nose, while Chanelle leans over toward Delahouère. Your speech was pretty good, but I thought you were supposed to mention my name, no? I alluded to it, Delahouère pleads, it seemed more effective. It's always better when it's subliminal. Whatever, Chanelle concedes, but what was that business about the value of sense, what got into you? I don't know, answers Delahouère, it just occurred to me. Anyway,

I don't think it sounds too bad as a slogan, and it shakes things up a bit.

Franck, by then, had taken the floor. His speech, which was to make an indelible mark on people's minds, would constitute a major turning point in the annals of the IPF, and more broadly in those of French politics. My dear friends, he pronounced very slowly, placing a silence after that vocative. The gravity of his statements was already perceptible, a historic page was about to turn, the audience held its breath, and I've now come to that moment.

23

AFTER Dorothée Lopez and Mike Brant, we could devote another mini-biography to Renée Hartevelt, a tall, beautiful Dutch woman, age twenty-five, studying comp. lit. at the University of Paris III.

On the afternoon of June 11, 1981, Renée Hartevelt went to see a Japanese friend of hers, age thirty-two, a pleasant young man, shy and well bred, like her a regular attendee of Henri Béhar's course on surrealism. Invoking an ongoing research project and his lack of knowledge of the German language, this young man of frail constitution—four foot nine, eighty-four pounds—asked her to record for him the poem "Abend" by Johannes Becher, an author little known in our climates even though he wrote the words to "Auferstanden aus Ruinen," the national anthem of the former East Germany, and Renée Hartevelt gladly accepted.

As she read this poem into a tape recorder, her back turned to the Japanese student, the latter picked up a .22LR rifle purchased the week before and killed Renée Hartevelt with a single blast to the back of the neck. That done, having more or less penetrated her postmortem—this point would never really be clarified—he cut off the tenderest parts of her body, stored about fifteen pounds of it in his refrigerator, and, for two days running, cooked most of it, by various methods, for his meals, sometimes with a side dish of peas. During those days, thirty-nine times over, he also photographed the evolution of the process—overall views of the corpse, close-ups of the removed organs, presentation of the dishes, etc.

On the morning of Saturday, June 13, for lack of a freezer and for the reasons one might imagine when the weather is hot, the Japanese student was forced to divest himself of Renée Hartevelt. Having cut up what remained of her into large chunks, he packed everything into two suitcases—head and torso in one, arms and legs in the other—which he stacked on a trolley before calling for a cab and then leaving his second-floor studio, laboriously dragging his load. It was after the arrival of this cab that my mother, this time returning from a shopping trip, noticed said young man, assisted by the driver, loading his suitcases into the trunk in front of his building, at no. 10 rue Erlanger.

In other words, closer to where I live today than was Mike Brant's place, and therefore closer to where my mother lived at the time, on the fringes of local events. But although she made the connection in the days that followed, from reading the paper after the young man had been arrested, my mother told me about it only much later. I was then in my eighth year, you know, too young and too sensitive to be informed about this type of occurrence.

From where I live, in any case, I haven't budged in the two days following the convening in Caen. And if I arrived late to this gathering, it was not at all my fault but Bardot's: we had agreed that he'd swing by to pick me up, but he got lost looking for rue Erlanger and took a fair amount of time finding it, then traffic was heavily congested around Porte d'Auteuil, after which, on the western highway, it opened up.

Bardot, then, parked in front of my building in his handsome, option-filled Audi Q2; I climbed in and sat next to him. He asked if I'd like any music and I said why not, he asked what kind and I said nothing special, he found an easy-listening station that he put on low volume, which provided the soundtrack all the way to Caen. After our lively exchange the other day, then its calmer conclusion, Bardot remained attentive, thoughtful, showing me how to adjust my seat for maximum comfort, calling me more insistently by my first name, for a moment I was afraid he was going to rest a hand on my knee, but no.

We exited the highway too soon, which forced us to cross an intermediate zone prior to Caen, where, like in all urban outskirts these days, names of businesses crushed against each other, sheltered by cursory constructions, identical and sans architectural ardor, that all looked provisional but alas were not. Bardot was explaining to me the ideological bases of the Independent Popular Federation, which sprang, if I understood correctly, from the widest smattering of Right and Left, not to mention a few detours via the Center. I didn't get much of it, but maybe, I said to myself, that was why their enterprise didn't seem to be doing so hot.

One could in fact observe a panoply of apparently contradictory penchants forming an uneven relief that careened from Anton Pannekoek to Georges Sorel, from Sixtus of Bourbon-Parma to Blanc de Saint-Bonnet, Bonald or Bordiga, Spencer, Thoreau, I didn't know those names, so meanwhile, without really listening, I itemized Carglass and Castorama, Optical Center and Kiloutou, Leroy Merlin, Office Depot, Monsieur Meuble, and Mr. Bricolage, then we arrived at the center of town and Bardot triple-parked in front of the

Convention Center. As a guy from security came running up to squabble over this choice of location, Bardot flashed a badge and things got sorted.

We approached the entrance. Bardot, preceding me, easily passed through the screening, but as I was about to follow him another guy in a calfskin windbreaker blocked my path, asking if I was a member, and I found the question immodest. Fragile in his calfskin, he was joined by another, stockier specimen in a mustard-colored jacket, who indicated to me that the meeting was reserved for adherents only, and I hesitated, not really wishing to join on the spur of the moment, without time to reflect. Fortunately, Bardot doubled back, pulling out his badge again and, as had to happen eventually, resting a hand on my shoulder. Then we entered the amphitheater.

On either side of the entrance, I recognized the two Asians who'd apprehended me among the agaves by Miss Tourneur's swimming pool. We glanced at each other, neither of them abandoning their composure, and I proceeded likewise. While I followed Bardot toward the front-row seats reserved for pooh-bahs, I noticed that a steely silence reigned in that hall, people seemed crystallized in their thoughts, I got the fish eye when my seat creaked as I sat down. As I then pondered the row of personalities seated onstage, I found I could identify nearly all of them, I had met most of them near Boucicaut, except for two or three I couldn't place; everyone was still and silent.

In the middle of that row, one of them finally stood up, whom I recognized as Chairman Franck Terrail, seen several days earlier, also near Boucicaut, waiting for an elevator. He was better dressed than at that time: classic slate-colored suit and bombyx-green tie, his Richelieu Havana captoes emitted rays. All around him, faces and postures were frozen in gravity.

Terrail took his time, then. My dear friends, he called us, and he took two or three deep breaths before continuing. I could feel that it would be a historic moment.

24

THE NEXT day, which is a Thursday, everyone reacts in their way to the speech Franck Terrail gave in Caen.

At around 7:30 a.m., Cedric Ballester wakes up in Louise Tourneur's room. As the latter is still asleep, Ballester leaves the bed quietly. The evening before, Louise and he talked late into the night about the new situation in the IPF, before—the former distracting from the latter—coupling more cursorily than usual.

Summary of the situation: while Louise doesn't want to accept the position of national secretary that Franck offered her during his speech in Caen, without quite knowing how to refuse (dilemma), Ballester, for his part, is split among his feelings for Louise, his fidelity to Franck, and his strategic allegiance to Chanelle (dilemma cubed).

He goes downstairs in his undershorts, makes coffee in the kitchen, swaps his civilian trunks for swimming ones, and crosses the terrace toward the pool, for despite the season the temperature is still favorable: a benign sun spreads over the cool water, in which Ballester swims for half an hour, hoping to dissolve his dilemma in chlorine but only frying his corneas. Pretending to catch his breath between two laps, he verifies out of the corner of his eye whether, in the villa next door, Dorothée Lopez might be watching him from her bedroom window, but he isn't too concerned: it's early, she's probably still sleeping.

Emerging from the basin, Ballester notes Apollodore Nguyen sitting alone before his *goban*, no doubt waiting for Ermosthenes to begin their first game of the day, which he prepared for by studying the reference text, attributed to Lee Chang-ho, titled *Invasion and Reduction*. Apollodore lifts an eyelid toward Ballester, the two men greet each other in silence. At this hour, all is silent, the air is troubled only by the humming of a Bentley Continental GT Speed's W123 engine along a path, under the faint cawing of blackbirds and crows.

Cedric Ballester has gone back up to the room where Louise, now awake, is talking on the phone to Dorothée Lopez, who has, in fact, been up for a long time, and who indeed was watching—not without troubled thoughts— Ballester swim from another window of her villa. She is now explaining to Louise in detail the precautions she would need to take to keep the party from splintering if, hypothetically, she were to accept the position of national secretary.

At around 10:45 a.m., in the apartment in Nelson Towers, Franck Terrail and Luigi Pannone are also taking stock of the political but mainly the sentimental situation. Although the morning is further along, the silence between their exchanges is also very present: one hears only the vague, diffuse noise of automobile and fluvial traffic down below on the quays, between the quays, beyond the quays.

Terrail seems devastated; Pannone tries to entertain him. Having prepared in the kitchen a reasonable breakfast—fruit salad, Greek yogurt, puffed rice—he brings it into the living room, but Terrail doesn't touch it. You have to eat something, Franck, lectures Pannone, you have to keep up your strength, and also move a bit now and then. At our age, you know, muscle loss. Did you make an appointment for your colo-noscopy? Yes, said Franck, I don't know. Pannone grimaces and tries another tack: Just look how nice it is outside, he exclaims, yanking open the curtains, doesn't weather like this just lift your spirits? Irruption into the living room of the sun, a ray of which splashes onto volumes of Elizabethan theater on the bottom left-hand shelves of the library, but Franck protests that the light is blinding and bad for the books, and Pannone draws the curtains shut with a sigh.

Do you think it could work? Franck worries for the sixth time that morning. The girl can't possibly refuse the position, Pannone affirms, in any case, she doesn't have a choice. I'm not talking about that, snaps Franck, I'm talking about her attitude toward me. I'm giving her total power, that's not something you can refuse, is it? It should bring us closer, don't you think? It could help her accept my feelings. No? Pannone remains silent. No? Franck insists. Have some more tea, Pannone suggests. Stay hydrated.

From 4:10 to 4:30 p.m., more or less, Joel Chanelle and Francis Delahouère talk on the phone, one being in the country and the other in town. Here, too, between utter-ances, a long pause settles in after they have once again commented on the Caen speech: the surprise nomination of Louise Tourneur and especially the dissolution of the executive committee, also announced by Terrail. They've made several decisions in reaction to this power grab; now they don't know what more to say, and fall silent. On the Delahouère side, somewhere around the Daumesnil neigh-borhood, all we can hear then is a child crying one floor up across the courtyard, and we also hear the mother of that child dumping twelve empty bottles into a trash bin in the back of said courtyard.

On the Chanelle side, in a country house in the Vexin region, the silence is disturbed only by the plaintive lowing of a cow behind a hedge, unless this lowing expresses joy, boredom, rut, or something else. Well, Chanelle supposes, looks like we've about covered it. I think so too, confirms Delahouère, shall we get together tomorrow to settle the details? No, says Chanelle, I've decided not to come into town, best for me to stay away for a few days. I don't want to be too mixed up in the operation, do you see? Not too physically present. I see, Delahouère understands, do as you think best.

But it's at precisely 7:56 p.m. that another young man, unknown until now, enters the scene, in yet another rural setting: Maxime Jaubert, twenty-three, with a master's degree in public policy and social regulation from Paris Dauphine University. And we're no longer in the Vexin but in the Tardenois.

Even more precisely, we're in the courtyard of a small manor house, where a huge, angular, margarine-colored Volvo, resembling an antiques dealer's station wagon and driven by Maxime Jaubert, has just pulled up slowly. On the back seat sits a lady who could be his mother, wearing a pink-and-gray athleisure ensemble by Stella McCartney, as well as sneakers with braided raffia soles. Young Jaubert, too—in a multi-zippered windbreaker, Chelsea boots, and coated denim jeans—is wearing a casual but costly outfit.

The Volvo comes to a gentle halt in front of the entrance to this edifice, and when Maxime Jaubert opens the driver's-side door, the cockpit is invaded by an amalgam of brutal agricultural stenches—diesel, tractor grease, fertilizer—emanating from the shed and other outbuildings, tempered by more soothing scents—humus, mushrooms, late-blooming roses—drifting in from the surrounding gardens and fields. When Jaubert cuts the headlights, it is very dark in the courtyard, everything is calm; the discreet purring of an electrical generator, a few furtive moths, and a vague insomniac dog in the distance merely enhance the ambient tranquility before a light goes on above an imposing door. The latter opens and a young woman named Léa Martineau appears, twenty-five years old, hooded down jacket and leggings, bachelor's in auditing and management control from the Business School Lausanne.

While Maxime Jaubert respectfully extracts a vanity case from the trunk, the lady steps out of the Volvo. All go well? asks Léa Martineau. Were you able to do some sightseeing? Wonderfully well, the lady simpers, we visited Fère-en-Tardenois. Ah, it's so pretty in Fère, Martineau assures her, there are things to see, the old market, and you saw the château, of course? We went by the château, the lady confirms, but naturally I remained in the car. Did you remember my shawl, Maxime? What a shame to have to leave, she continues, I would have loved to spend a few more days here. A real vacation. The fresh air has done me a world of good, but I think it's time to go back. Is everything ready for my return, Léa? Everything's all set, Nicole, Martineau reassures her. Good, the lady says. We go into action the day after tomorrow.

25

EVERYONE trembles, so it seems, at the very mention of Mozzigonacci. Apparently you need only to speak his name to poison the atmosphere. But they're wrong, they're mistaken, they're imagining things about Jean-Loup Mozzigonacci, who is now having lunch, peacefully, as every day, in a moderately priced café-restaurant on rue Ternaux, just downstairs from his apartment. He is a stocky sexagenarian of average height and with close-cropped hair, bright eyes behind frameless glasses, wearing cotton trousers, a navy blue sweater threadbare at the elbows and with buttons on the shoulder, and sandals with straps, who looks anything but chilling.

Mozzigonacci's benevolent habitus, his affable, not to say affectionate, manner, might suggest those of a former summer camp director or defrocked team chaplain. If he is, as they intimate, a man of radical solutions, his appearance lets none of this show. His body language is calm, his expression candid, and he seems to be well liked in this establishment, where he is apparently a regular, speaking familiarly to the staff and even to the clientele, a friendly remark for each and the same smile for all, except for Bloch-Besnard, in whose company, side by side, he has just finished his lunch.

They order two coffees, then a third on the arrival of Delahouère, who sits opposite them. So, my dear Francis, Mozzigonacci cheerily apostrophizes, is tonight the big night?

So many questions still to settle, sighs Delahouère. Their brief subsequent comments remain vague generalities, and during this exchange Bloch-Besnard abstains from intervening. Shall we go? Mozzigonacci finally suggests, signaling the waitress. Leave it, Francis, I've got this.

We rejoin them by the stairs, which they climb and which are a microcosm of the building as a whole: modest but brightly lit and well maintained, well polished, no graffiti, no abandoned pails, no floor mats askew. No elevator, either, which Mozzigonacci wouldn't need anyway since he lives on the second floor, before reaching which they are joined by Jean-François Bardot, running up behind them. They enter a studio of about 320 square feet, Mozzigonacci's aerie, which hasn't had a fresh coat of paint since the Gulf War, maybe even the Six-Day War, while the panes of its two windows looking out on the street haven't been washed since, let's say, the beginning of the last Donbas war.

It's just that that foxhole exudes a somewhat military atmosphere, ascetic and dated: narrow bed made with hospital corners, metal desk supporting a battered verdigris IBM Selectric typewriter, tubular armchair and two mess hall chairs against a wall. Sanitary-wise, a hot plate and a sink serve as kitchen and bathroom, and as for leisure and sports, there are an old brushed-silver Thomson VCR and a horizontal bar bolted to the ceiling. Three shelves hold fifty-odd volumes covered in brown or glassine paper; two undershirts, one tan, one blue, hang from a wire above the oil-filled radiator. Nothing on the wall but, under glass, a vocational certificate for airborne troops encircled by a pennant, a rosette, and three faded group photos. The overall effect is austere and modest: if Jean-Loup Mozzigonacci wields any power, it is certainly not financial.

The man takes his seat in the stiff armchair, turns to Delahouère and Bardot, in the mess hall chairs, and to Bloch-Besnard, sitting with the edge of his butt on the edge of the bed. They seem to be waiting only for young Brandon Labroche, and the latter soon arrives, his little round hat squatting on his head; he inspects the unavailable chairs, then, not daring to occupy the other edge of the bed, leans against the wall at attention under the certificate. I believe we're all here, smiles Mozzigonacci. So then, what do you need from me?

Ideas, blurts Delahouère. It's just that this business of the national secretary, you see what I mean, he develops. Joel wants to keep little Louise from getting the job, the whole thing stinks. Chanelle could have come to talk to me himself, Mozzigonacci points out. He's resting, says Delahouère, he's exhausted by all this. But if the girl gets to be secretary, our whole operation is compromised. And no need to remind you that, in that case, your influence is in danger. I thought she didn't want the job, Mozzigonacci knits his brow. You can't turn a thing like that down, laments Delahouère, she's playing hard to get but she'll come around, we know what they're like, they always come around. And if Franck insists on nominating her, we're screwed.

There follow several historical examples, arguments, and situations illustrating this established fact, too technical to be related here, and during the uttering of which you can hear various street noises, clearly audible from the second floor: scraps of conversation, babbles of infant, shouts of voice, slams of door, bleats of horn, rumbling of motors much less distinguished than those at the Tourneur-Lopez compound, the vehicles circulating around rue Ternaux generally belonging to a more middling class.

So, in short, those are the facts, Delahouère summarizes,

we're at an impasse. We're stuck as long as Franck's in charge. I can see where you're heading, Francis, Bloch-Besnard implies. I'm not heading anywhere, Delahouère huffs, I'm explaining. I'm elucidating.

He continues to elucidate, insinuating in conclusion that Chairman Franck Terrail, like it or not, well, it would be good if he were around a little less. By whatever method, they would be better off removing him. I don't mean physically, of course, but, well. You mean that physically wouldn't be a bad thing either? ventures Bloch-Besnard. Raising an eyebrow, the psychiatrist Bardot also seems to be perking up an ear. There's that, Delahouère admits, we could also look at it from that angle. Note, I haven't said anything, but sometimes there are, if I may say so, decisions that... He doesn't finish the sentence.

They fall silent before such a prospect. Bardot, pensive, looks elsewhere. Brandon Labroche looks shifty and brushes off his sleeve. Bloch-Besnard and Delahouère look dour. The hour is grave, and even the noises from rue Ternaux are suspended for an instant, as if surprised, or personally concerned. Only Mozzigonacci seems to react more casually to the hypothetical, let's not mince words, liquidation of Franck Terrail. He appears amused, as if it were just a funny idea, incongruous but entertaining, like someone inviting him to a picnic in a water-treatment plant or a weekend on a sewage farm. And besides, when you get down to it, why not.

But he pulls himself together: It's true that Franck is inconsistent, he diagnoses, and we'd be better off without him. That said, it's delicate, he's still very popular. Did you see the ovation he got after the Caen speech? Even the financial papers reported on it. Exactly, Delahouère jumps in, that's what's good about it. If he disappears, everything collapses, and if everything collapses, a good solid takeover becomes much more plausible. Crowds are irrational in grief, mourning can turn into all kinds of things. That's not false, Bardot testifies clinically. I hear what you're saying, Mozzigonacci opines, joining his fingertips together pensively beneath his chin. As far as I'm concerned, I wouldn't be opposed, but I couldn't handle it personally. I could take care of it, young Labroche intervenes. Shut up, Brandon, Bloch-Besnard orders under his breath.

What we'd need for this are professionals, Mozzigonacci elaborates, and I no longer have many contacts in that area, the few younger guys I knew in private practice aren't in France anymore. They've all gone to hot spots like South Sudan, Somalia, Yemen, who knows. The only ones I still see occasionally are retirees. Never you fear, Jean-Loup, Delahouère reassures him, we'll take care of it, I just wanted to get your opinion. Of course, there's still the matter of logistics. Does anyone have any ideas? How about you, Jean-François, got any suggestions? I've had one, answers Bardot, for a while now.

26

WHEN HE called me the next morning, I was at my window, where I often—very often—go to stand when I have nothing better to do. I was waiting for something new to happen in rue Erlanger, anything would do, but I'm all too aware that nothing ever does: it isn't every day that a crooner hurls himself from one of its balconies, or a pampered Asian scion ingests a blond student. I have no doubt that other succinct existences have played out on this street, like anywhere else, but sadly they don't offer the same scenic interest. Still, if there's one life that came very close to being abridged, it's that of rue Erlanger itself, in 1942, and here I'll place an open parenthesis.

On June 4 of that year, Captain Paul Sézille, general secretary of the Institute for the Study of Jewish Questions, located at no. 21 rue La Boétie, Paris 8th, wrote to SS-Hauptsturmführer Theodor Dannecker, director of Section IV J of the Gestapo, to express his dissatisfaction. In his letter, Captain Sézille explained that, as he saw it, it was nonsensical to ask honest Frenchmen to identify Jews by their wearing a yellow star if you didn't also inform the poor unfortunates about Paris streets that bore Jewish names. Joined to this missive was a list of the thirty-odd thoroughfares in question that he suggested renaming—boulevard Pereire notably becoming, in the captain's overactive brain, boulevard Édouard Drumont. Among these streets figured, for instance, on the Right Bank, rues Halévy, Mendelssohn, Meyerbeer, Chernoviz, Florence Blumenthal, and Erlanger. This plan was not followed up on, and Sézille was somehow ousted from his institute. Rue Erlanger had a narrow escape, and here I'll close my parentheses, but it's always the same problem with parentheses: when you close them, like it or not you find yourself back in the sentence, and the sentence is, indeed, relating that Bardot called me the next morning.

He had changed his tone again since the other day, it was less haughty than in his consulting room but also distinctly less friendly than on the western highway. Listen, Gerard—he nonetheless kept calling me by my forename—we really should get together soon. Having nothing better to do, as I said, I readily agreed and offered to come by rue du Louvre in the next few days. It would be better to meet up at my place, he interrupted, and not in the next few days but right now. I live in the suburbs but it's not hard to get to, near Chatou, I don't know if you know it. Yes, Chatou, I knew it more or less, a fairly prosperous sector, it didn't surprise me overmuch, I said fine.

Not hard, sure, but it took me a good hour on the RER A and then on Bus B and then on foot in the cold. In his fur coat, Bardot was waiting for me as arranged at the corner of rue Beaugendre and rue du Général Leclerc, then we had to walk down an alley stemming off rue Beaugendre and there you go, he informed me, here we are. Bardot's home was a charming 1930s residence, two huge floors, a pretty ivy-clad facade, tall plane trees behind and hollyhocks in front; it exuded affluence but I didn't have time for much of a look.

We went inside, me following behind. We'll go to my

office, Bardot indicated. We walked quick-time through a large living room in which, on a wing chair, a decorative woman was nursing a chubby baby: My wife, Bardot subtitled without stopping. The wife nodded at my passage, pulling a shawl over her chest, from which dangled the chub; I bowed as I walked past her while not staring, these movements took some coordination, we arrived in what seemed like an office. As I was about to sit down, Bardot made a sign not to, while taking off his coat. We're going downstairs, he said, I want to show you something. Where could we go downstairs to, I worried, given that we were on the ground floor?

I found myself in a vast cellar fitted out as a projection room; it was very dark and it took my eyes some time to adjust: three rows of plush red seats, three walls and a floor of polished concrete, the fourth wall occupied by a screen the dimensions of a king-size mattress. A console equipped with lights and buttons was set up before a seat in the front row, where Bardot took his place. I took one next to him.

I do a bit of moviemaking on the side, he explained. Please forgive me if it's not terribly sophisticated technically, I'm counting on your indulgence. He pressed one of the buttons, further blackening the space, and, turning toward me: I want to show you a little film that might interest you—he smiled; you couldn't see a thing, but I could distinctly hear his smile in the darkness—you'll see. He must have pressed another button, as the film immediately started. And then I indeed saw.

The setting reminded me of something, but I couldn't quite recall what. A room, a closet in which hang women's clothes, a desk with two drawers. Close-up of one of the drawers, open and full of papers. A hand enters the scene, riffles through the papers. It's not very well framed, the poorly lit image trembles a bit, clearly amateur work. After the shot of the desk drawer, a door left ajar opens onto a bathroom, dark at first, then the lights snap on. Cut. Tilt shot of a washing machine, the camera jerkily pans left and we make out a person sitting in a chair against that machine. Zoom onto that person, whose head we don't see, encased as it is in a yellow plastic bag. The camera pulls back, and then what I saw was myself.

I saw myself first from the rear, then three-quarters rear, then my face was easily recognizable when I turned around, and I have to say, I understand when actors claim they don't like seeing themselves on-screen. It was the first time this had happened to me, but yes, I get their point. I found myself ugly, poorly dressed, as hunched as my diameter would allow, everything that displeases me in myself became hateful, then the question of my appearance quickly became secondary, for what could be seen about me more specifically was that I was gripping a knife.

It was when I looked at myself holding that knife, with its red handle and differently red blade, my eyes shifting from that utensil to the encased person, that I remembered the scene. The house of a certain La Mothe-Marlaux. The day when I stumbled onto the body of the dead woman, before panicking and fleeing. I must have buried that episode deep in my memory, as it was almost forgotten, had vanished, or was located in a very distant past, whereas it had happened only two weeks earlier. And now there was a stable long shot in which I had the starring role, I was stock-still, contemplating the victim of a killing, with the murder weapon in my hand. You might find the scene absurd; you might also judge it to be damning.

I sat there watching, I would have liked to have seen the rest and even for the film to continue, for it never to end, for it to go on eternally in order to postpone what was doubtless to follow. But it ended just as abruptly, the screen went black, and I remained there without reacting, occupied by one incongruent thought: At least the film was silent. I understood how unpleasant it is to see yourself against your will, but it seems it's even worse to also hear your voice.

I was at that point in my thoughts, this time, when Bardot's voice wrested me out of them. I don't think, he judged, that I need to paint you a picture.

27

SILENT though it was, the film had somehow deafened me. During its projection, I was so wrapped up in the spectacle that the intensity of my vision, entirely concentrated on it, must have disconnected my other sensory equipment. Only after the fact did I vaguely become aware that the silence, during those few minutes, had not been absolute: there were slight, irregular noises behind me, like faint, intermittent whispers, plus a stifled titter. But, too absorbed in what I was seeing, I hadn't thought to turn around.

When the lights came back on and Bardot told me a picture wasn't necessary, after the first moment of shock it was urgent to react, and I immediately said I wasn't going along with it. I nervously stated that I wasn't going along with it. I feverishly articulated, forcing a snicker, that no way was I going along with it. I might be easily intimidated by nature, but I played the guy who doesn't get taken in just like that: I argued that it was a blatant setup, it was ridiculous—that's where I forced my forced laugh—that it didn't make any sense, had nothing to do with me, they weren't going to leave me holding the bag. As the murmurs had started up again, I glanced backward and saw two guys sitting in the last row but didn't linger on them.

It might not make any sense, agreed Bardot, except the woman on the chair was quite dead. Have some respect for the deceased, if you please, Gerard, and keep in mind that your fingerprints on the knife are clear as can be. Correct me if I'm wrong, but I believe your prints were taken at the time of your incident on the Paris–Zurich flight, not so? I imagine they're still on file. He smiled again. He could see he'd scored a hit.

Now that we've established this, he noted, we can move on to the business at hand. Then, turning toward the two guys in back: I think you can leave us, gentlemen. I turned as well, looked at the two of them more closely. I didn't recognize them at first, as they had changed quite a bit. When I finally placed them, I understood fully. I might have known.

The first one was, of course, the old man who had hired me to find his Janine and paid with a rubber check. Except that he now struck me as much less aged, more relaxed, much healthier and stronger, wearing a light blue sweatshirt and Havana-brown chinos instead of his antique corseted suit; even his hair had grown since our last encounter. No surprise, then, that the other was the so-called La Mothe-Marlaux in person, apart from the fact that he, as if via the principle of communicating vessels, had conversely shrunk: there was no trace of the degenerate upper bourgeois I had met, no more signet ring or ascot; he seemed deteriorated, breathless, and pale, his whispers from before denoted not so much discretion as respiratory distress. Both of them must have accepted this job for lack of better. Thus goes the life of theatrical bit players, forced to accept this type of walk-on when the screen, the stage, and even TV soap operas no longer want any part of them.

The two fifth-rate actors stood up, headed for the door, and I remained alone with Bardot. You've taken a lot of trouble, doctor, I attempted to mock. I try to prepare, he admitted, which is why I now have a hold over you. Wasted effort, I again attempted to object, this business about a dead woman doesn't hold up. Whether it holds up or not, he replied warmly, I've got something else in reserve. Do you remember more specifically that Paris–Zurich flight, when you were still an attendant? At that point, I again distinctly felt not so good.

You managed to get off pretty lightly at the time, he continued, but I did a little digging, things on that flight didn't go quite the way you claimed, am I right? You can't prove a thing, I muttered, looking at the tips of my fingers. Just that sentence condemns you, Bardot guffawed. And besides, you're forgetting that you told me all about it in minute detail during our little sessions, don't you remember?

I recalled that, indeed, in a moment of weakness, taking Bardot for a normal practitioner bound by doctor–patient confidentiality, I had spilled quite a lot about that Zurich flight, its painful consequences having resulted in my dismissal as well as the addition of my name to a blacklist. I thought, at the time, that he wasn't listening and even that he didn't give a flip, but it would have been smarter of me to keep my mouth shut. In short, Bardot concluded, let's just say that I've got you by the balls, I'd even say by several pairs of them. You will therefore do point for point what I tell you to do, Fulmard. So he was no longer calling me by my forename.

He exposed his plan: He offered to destroy the film, forget about the Paris–Zurich incident, and pay me to boot, even handsomely. In exchange for which I had to do him a favor, and not just a small one: take care of somebody, by his lights. It was, he assured me, a very simple task and everything was all set, I was running absolutely no risk, and here was the tool to do it. He pulled out something wrapped in a cloth from under the console, unfolded the cloth, I saw the something, it was of compact size. Take it in your hand, Bardot encouraged me. I took it.

Obviously, it was a weapon, a handgun, to be exact. After the knife, now we had a gun. When you get down to it, I find them tiring, all these stories about firearms. Why do there always have to be guns in these stories, I mused. It's conventional, tedious, unsurprising, but whatever, I suppose it's a requisite feature. Check it out, Bardot insisted, familiarize yourself with it.

It was a small black object, barely the size of my hand, with the words EKOL & VOLTRAN TUNA engraved along the barrel and a red dot under the safety catch. I found it rather light and said so. Sixteen point five ounces, Bardot specified, made in Istanbul. A modified gas pistol, he explained, initially only dissuasive, but any milling machine can make it capable of firing real bullets, he kept elaborating, by boring the barrel to insert a 7.65 mm tube with no exhaust hole. None of this meant anything to me, but Bardot explained the advantage: the weapon being for unrestricted sale pretty much everywhere, no registration required, the police would have no way of tracing it. No one's the wiser. Fine, I interrupted, but who is this somebody? The one you want me to—You'll know soon enough, Bardot cut in, as if it were a mere bagatelle. You'll get a photo.

We went back up to the ground floor, first to his office, where he handed me back the tool, which I slipped into my pocket. Since he offered to see me out, we crossed the living room in the other direction. In a corner of his playpen, the chubby baby was dozing, Madame Bardot was snoring lightly in front of a televised fiction. The few images I saw in passing indicated a rerun of a show from the '80s, and I caught only four words of dialogue: "Oh really? Two months?"

At the door of his house, Bardot handed me a fat envelope that supposedly contained the promised cash—There's a lot there, he reminded me, you'll need it—which I slipped into my other pocket. He told me to expect the photo, then let me leave; as I returned to rue Erlanger, my two pockets weighed nearly the same.

28

BUILT around 1540 and renovated from 1865 to 1869, Bavelaer Manor is composed of a fourteen-room primary dwelling, a groundskeeper's cottage, and several outbuildings —stables, barn, granary, sheds. Surrounded by a seventeen-acre park with a stream running through it, this tall, massive construction is registered in the supplemental inventory of historic monuments even if no one ever visits it. In fact, it seems people prefer to avoid it, as if its toothlike profile, its dull coloring, and its steep-walled appearance impose silence, or maybe suspicion.

Sixty miles east of Paris, a freezing night paralyzes the Tardenois, a small, hilly region with a dense hydrographic network, where, isolated between two bluffs and blurred by fog, stands the Bavelaer edifice. Corpulent and flanked by turrets capped in slate, it is reached via a sinuous path surrounded by grasslands, peat, and groves. All is now gloomy and quiet, the manor's facade is dark, overlooking a square courtyard where two cars are parked side by side: a Volvo station wagon of venerable vintage and an Opel Crossland in used condition. With its shutters closed, the interior of the building is opaque, like the cockpits of these vehicles, whose windows are obscured by condensation.

At around five ten, one window on the ground floor lights up: moving shadow on yellow square. The shadow belongs to Maxime Jaubert, who is busy in the kitchen with a coffeepot and a toaster. After buttering the toast, he switches on a radio, squeezes a few oranges, goes to scramble some eggs, opens the window a crack, and immediately shuts it again.

Regarding the light, day is still a long way off, but, as said day is predicted to be rainy, not much will be visible of the surroundings for a good while yet. As for sound, through the briefly opened window one could hear tingings of porcelain, glass, and metal, the radio crackling fresh news at low volume, then an echo of steps lighter than Jaubert's, and here comes Léa Martineau.

She and Maxime Jaubert exchange a few words, disappear with trays, then three other adjacent windows light up, those of an ample library tiled in gray-and-white marble, garnished with fake medieval furniture, and framed by two fireplaces with overmantel mirrors bearing coats of arms. While Jaubert lays out the breakfast items on the center table, Léa Martineau goes out and comes back five minutes later, followed by Nicole Tourneur herself, Nicole Tourneur in person, to all appearances in fine fettle, wearing a downy dressing gown with a hood. They sit down, they offer one another the coffeepot, they chat in low voices, they divvy up the scrambled eggs, it seems that more than once they tell a joke, they pass the salt.

At a quarter to six, while Maxime Jaubert clears the table, Léa Martineau escorts the national secretary to her room. There, in front of a mirror, they put the finishing touches on her appearance, which is intended, contrary to the classically flattering aims of the cosmetic arts, to make her look raw, worn down, malnourished, without the slightest artifice, as if at the end of a long and painful sequestration. For the past three days, Nicole Tourneur has made sure not to wash her hair, which Léa Martineau musses a bit more for the occasion, accentuating the bags under her eyes and deepening her wrinkles with a brush, then Tourneur puts on the same pathetic sportswear she wore in the videos, Martineau having fouled it a bit more.

At six thirty, they climb into the Opel, Jaubert and Martineau in front, Nicole Tourneur hidden under a blanket in the back seat, the headlights make out a stretch with no surprises all the way to Château-Thierry: fields to the right, copses to the left, hazy forest profiles in the background. No surprise, either, that the weather hasn't improved: it drizzles on and off, the visibility isn't great, on top of which they're freezing.

Aren't we setting off kind of early? Martineau yawns. It's critical that we arrive before nine, Jaubert reminds her, and I don't like taking chances. The paper gets put to bed at ten thirty, which leaves plenty of time for them to give us the front page. But you never know with the highway, if there's an accident or something and it jams up. His concern is unfounded: after they turn onto the eastern highway at the Château-Thierry tollbooth, traffic flows freely as day breaks at the approach to Paris.

We're here. From a bird's-eye view, Porte de Bercy resembles an intestinal tract, the playfield of a Gottlieb pinball machine, or a loosely tied Borromean knot. This huge transit zone is a jumble of tangled bypasses and interchanges where fast lanes crisscross, join, and superimpose, and among which vegetal areas subsist, herbescent and sparsely wooded, shaped like crescents, trapezoids, or triangles, vague islands inaccessible to pedestrian mortals.

After having, at ten minutes to nine, furtively deposited

Nicole Tourneur on one of those islets, a strip of grass crammed among three lanes, Maxime Jaubert extricates himself from the maze to regain the normal roadways of the twelfth arrondissement. As soon as he can, to wit, on a service road off boulevard Poniatowski, he parks the Opel, takes from his pocket a new prepaid mobile phone bought at a tobacconist's in Fère-en-Tardenois, successively dials the numbers of the newspaper *Le Monde* and Agence France-Presse. To the first persons who answer, he dictates a brief text before hanging up, placing this phone on the ground and mashing it under his bootheel, then throwing the debris into the nearest manhole. And they're off, it seems. They're bound to make a splash.

29

BUT IT didn't work out as well as they'd hoped.

After the Internal Security functionaries urgently retrieved Nicole Tourneur from her scrap of interchange, they transported her for observation to Clamart, where an army training hospital occasionally welcomed handpicked civilian personalities. She underwent a battery of tests that revealed nothing out of the ordinary, alternating with interviews led by other functionaries that revealed nothing further, Tourneur sticking obstinately to the same story: still sequestered in the same place, yes; well treated, yes; able to identify her kidnappers, no. The police officers finally gave up, had her sign a discharge to leave the Percy hospital but, rather than letting her go back home, recommended that she stay elsewhere, as a precaution and for a while.

They therefore transferred her by ambulance to a safe house with a hotel demeanor, belonging to the Ministry of the Interior, that acts as a shelter for notables under surveillance: four plainclothesmen relieve each other in permanent rotation in the lobby, while three draftees from the 35th Belfort Infantry Regiment cool their heels on the sidewalk. Each resident has a comfortable room with room service and a view of the garden, access to a gym on the top floor, a driver at their disposal.

What really didn't work was the effect Nicole Tourneur

hoped to produce with these simulacra of kidnapping and release. She who dreamed of shaking up the political spheres, civil society, the international press, and thereby relaunching her popularity, had to admit it was a flop. Naturally her return was reported in the papers, but in news in brief rather than front-page headlines, less in the declarative mode than in the conditional, then commented on half-heartedly for a few days, but like anything else it didn't last. It lasted even less long in that reactions from the political class were all but nonexistent, no one wishing to grant any importance to the latest doings of the IPF, a minor formation that they fully intended to keep that way. Launched on the social networks by the Jaubert-Martineau couple was a vague rumor that Nicole Tourneur was refusing all interviews, photographs, and public appearances, but the fact was that no one had asked for any, that the public had soon tired of the whole affair, and that at bottom no one gave a shit.

Even within the party, the reception was polarized, which is understandable: those who were getting used to Nicole's disappearance, nourishing their private ambitions on her absence, found themselves in an awkward position. Franck Terrail and Joel Chanelle preferred to keep silent, and Francis Delahouère barely managed to eke out a cursory press release: Deeply affected by what she has just suffered, our national secretary must take several weeks of rest. We are certain that everyone can understand how trying this ordeal has been and, with all due discretion, will respect this moment.

In short, they isolated her and here she is, poor Tourneur, all alone for the past five days in this room, where, tired of leafing through the papers that have already stopped mentioning her, fed up with tapping away on her remote control when all the channels have forgotten her, she ponders through the window a garden desiccated by frost. She, who until now has lived only for the spotlight, often neglecting her own daughter, is trying for the twentieth time since her return to call said daughter, but in vain: it's always busy, or else she gets voicemail. As she tries one more time without Louise's mobile or landlines ever picking up, a sense of guilt grips Nicole Tourneur, melancholy sets in, discouragement overwhelms her. She finds the time passing slowly, she is languishing, she is nodding off, as are we: so let's pick up the pace.

Tourneur calls the main desk. Orders a car. Crosses the lobby, climbs into the vehicle—a Hyundai hybrid—gives the driver Louise's address. The Hyundai starts up, followed at fifty yards by a Lexus containing in its back seat two staff members of the establishment, not displeased to get a change of air. They arrive at the residential bunker, Tourneur gets out of the Hyundai. Walks toward the blockhouse adjoining the entrance gate, the guard has a blank look when he sees her, pretends not to recognize her, then to recognize her after a slight delay, ends up smiling at her with deference or commiseration, hard to tell which. Opens the gate. Silence in the drive paths, a thicker silence than usual, we don't hear any purring of deluxe motors or hoarse cries of birds. The sky is gray, the air dry and powdery, Tourneur shivers. The staff members have remained near the entrance, cozy and warm in their Lexus.

Nicole Tourneur arrives at her daughter's house. The house appears locked. The garden looks abandoned, the agaves bordering the pool are dusty and neglected, even their tips and spines are dull. One of the Nguyen brothers, unshaven, cigarette dangling from his lips and sweatsuit wrinkled, equipped with a hoop net and a vacuum, is cleaning the murky water of the pool, on whose surface float numerous leaves, twigs, and dead insects, with a belly-up field mouse. Tourneur questions this Nguyen brother but he doesn't have the faintest idea, no, where Miss Louise might be. You could try next door, he suggests, at Madame Lopez's. But Dorothée Lopez's villa appears just as locked down, shutters closed, flyers sticking out of the mailbox, weeds eating away at the lawn, over which the other Nguyen brother, looking equally slovenly, tugs a desultory rake. Similarly questioned by Tourneur, the other brother proves equally evasive about Madame Lopez, no idea where she might be, either.

And yet they do know, but they have their instructions. Upon her mother's release, Louise Tourneur felt harassed. A panic-stricken Franck Terrail began bombarding her with increasingly ardent phone calls, Louise ended up not answering, in desperation Franck sent emissaries, first young Flax and then even Luigi Pannone; Louise Tourneur received them once, slammed the door on them from then on. As they persisted nonetheless, Louise decided to leave, flee, go as far away as possible—ordered her servants to keep their mouths shut—accompanied by Ballester and chaperoned by Dorothée Lopez. Destination: Sulawesi.

But tell me, now, what *is* Sulawesi, and wherever might it be located? Well, this place is in fact far away, really very far away, midway between the Maluku Islands and Borneo. It's a large island composed of four peninsulas whose outline suggests that of a limping spider, a deconstructed star, or a slightly diluted lowercase *k*: there is plenty there to afford you a tranquil little spot. Its climate is tropical, its overall landscape hilly, its flora and fauna profuse, and three seas shimmy at your feet.

With Lopez on their heels, Louise Tourneur and Cedric

Ballester thus settled on Sulawesi, more precisely in the village of Bira, located at the southeastern tip of the southern peninsula. They stopped at the Amatoa Resort, where they occupied the deluxe Honeymoon Suite while Lopez made do with a room one floor down, less vast but still not bad. From their balcony, finally in peace, they pondered the Flores Sea below them. Turning around, they saw tall mountains capped with mist, among which, via narrow corridors, torrents surged across the rainforest from one waterfall to the next to finally explode on the shore, gush in a stream along immaculate sandy beaches fringed with sandalwood, teak, and coconut.

And so, after the business with the firearm, a requisite feature of this type of story, as Gerard Fulmard pertinently observed, now we're getting some exoticism. To tick every box, the only thing missing is a sex scene—but a real sex scene, of course, artfully described, less depressing and thwarted than Franck Terrail's in Pigalle. We'll see about that later. Let's keep it in reserve should the opportunity arise.

30

SUCH A scene, moreover, could occur even now, for everything in the Honeymoon Suite lends itself to it: the ambience and air-conditioning are muted, the colors are calming, the vaporous veils filter a soft light, and especially the round bed, of senatorial dimensions, upholstered in buffalo hide and at the foot of which lies a tray laden with cool drinks, would jibe perfectly. It would be all the more suitable in that at first we would make out only the frolics of silhouettes blurred by the mosquito netting, an effective intro before indulging in close-ups and extreme close-ups, the better to follow the succession of postures, harmonized by the surf from the Flores Sea down below, the comings and goings of its waves providing an excellent soundtrack, symmetrical and synchronous with the action.

But no, it's eleven in the morning, it's already been a while since Louise Tourneur and Cedric Ballester finished breakfast on the balcony, and we missed the scene, assuming it took place at all, in any case we've come too late, maybe another time. Meanwhile, beneath their SPF 50, Cedric and Louise are getting some sun in their deck chairs while vaguely planning, in languid and often unfinished sentences, the day's itinerary.

Various options are available to fill this itinerary, which, as it's been only three days since their arrival, they are far from having exhausted. There's the beach option, a beach that one approaches via a narrow path that zigzags down the hillside and that, widening in a delta at its lower end, reaches the seashore like an opening fan. This option then subdivides into a triple sub-option: you have simple bathing, scuba diving, or guided snorkeling—instructors as well as the equipment appropriate for these endeavors are available at the hotel. There is the related option of the infinity pool located below the balcony, from which one enjoys between breaststrokes a panoramic view of the sapphire-blue sea. There's the visit to the old village, the excursion into the jungle—its interlacing vines and rare species—which is within reach as soon as one leaves the hotel, where forest guides stand ready at the residents' disposal. There is also the option of staying on the balcony and not doing squat, calmly tanning and putting off any decisions until later, with Dorothée, who will surely have some good ideas: she should be here any minute, let's wait for her to have lunch.

This is not taking into account the fact that, given the time difference, not to mention her natural bent, Dorothée Lopez has gotten into the habit of rising extremely late since their arrival in Sulawesi. This morning, for instance, even when the aperitif hour has chimed, even after the hour of lunch, Lopez still hasn't appeared: they'll start without her, they ring, a bellboy appears with a menu—gado-gado salad with peanut sauce, bushmeat with sambal on a bed of agar-agar—Ballester nods, the boy sets the table.

The salad isn't bad, but while attacking the bushmeat, Louise Tourneur's hand fumbles and her knife slips: the blade scratches the inner surface of her left index finger, at the webbing between the first two digits: slight pain, muffled cry, pearl of blood, it's nothing. It's nothing, but it's bleeding a bit all the same, and Cedric immediately grabs Louise's hand, takes her index into his mouth to stanch the flow, then keeps it between his lips longer than is necessary, envelops it with his tongue while gazing at Louise with a half-closed eye: this might finally be the start of our explicit scene, the ideal foreplay, it would be entirely possible, but no, foiled again, the scene is interrupted by the clamorous incursion of Dorothée Lopez.

Lopez has arrived executing a dance step, lifting her arms above her head and clacking her heels while yodeling in a super-shrill register, no doubt to make known her happiness at being there. She has shown up in a sarong so polychromatic that it makes your eyes water; coiffed in a turban with tropical motifs and with a frangipani flower behind her ear; shod in flip-flops; and adorned with an artisanal necklace bought three days earlier, at thirty times the normal price, at the airport in Makassar. They've straightened themselves up, they've greeted her, they've invited her to sit.

So what can we get up to today? Lopez marvels while clapping her hands. You have any ideas? Ballester, in order to reply, must extract from his mouth Louise's index finger, which he presents to Dorothée. What's that, she frets. Just a minute. My glasses. Which she puts on while leaning over Louise's hand, then removes once the latter has been examined: Nothing serious, she drops the subject, no need for a Band-Aid, it'll heal by itself. Maybe a bit of disinfectant, and even then. So what are we getting up to?

Well, we could take a little spin around the jungle, she proposes after a moment's thought, there's one of Dorothée's good ideas. They concur, they stand, and they head, full of enthusiasm and flanked by a guide named Budiman, into the heart of the forest primeval, mysterious, and savage that is located two steps away: let us enter that jungle, shadowy and damp, sepulchral, trembling, rustling, a faunistic and floral treasure.

But first, they're not going to see much of that fauna. Of course, they will perk up their ears when Budiman raises a delighted finger, pointing to the indistinct bowels of the forest from which emanate the vague bellows, barks, and distant whistles of, they try hard to believe, dwarf buffaloes and hog deer, whose existence they've read about in the guidebook. True, they glimpse a couple of old black monkeys with long proboscises, but they are lacking in suppleness, a bit stooped, and seem to be quietly returning home; they don't want to bother them. Craning their necks toward the canopy, they labor to see hypothetical birds of paradise, but ultimately make out only three surrogate pigeons who have strayed into the sector and keep their distance; they didn't bring binoculars. As a last resort, Budiman tries to communicate his enthusiasm at the sight of old excrement that, he assures them (they seem to understand), was left there by a white tiger.

Second, as to flora, there aren't that many vines, the ferns and rubber trees look poorly watered, the orchids are wilted, the succulents have no more style than in an orthodontist's waiting room, they start to drag their heels. Budiman gathers that they're somewhat disappointed, out of desperation he tries to draw their attention to a spiderweb that he declares to be exceptional, but they've already seen plenty like that, those spiderwebs: they pretend to be interested all the same, they smile for his benefit, in any case they have no idea what he's going on about in Tomini-Tolitoli. Perhaps, too, he has lingered on this phenomenon mainly to distract their attention while he quietly picks up a crumpled Kleenex, left by the previous tourists, that compromises the virginity of the place. Now, as they turn around and catch him in the act, Budiman makes a sheepish face before stating proudly, they think they understand, that above all one must protect the environment.

An hour passes, Budiman ultimately realizes they're getting fed up and that they've had quite enough; that it's too hot, too humid; and that, while there are no sensational animals, there are on the other hand insects of all stripes constantly sneaking toward your orifices, you have to watch your feet for possible snakes, nervously avoid the clumps of carnivorous plants with voluptuous profiles that stretch languorously onto your path. When Budiman declares that it's time to go back, despite the linguistic barrier they understand him with relief. They return to the hotel to take a rest, propose meeting up again at the beach a little later, toward the end of the afternoon? Great. See you then.

31

THE BEACH is nice. Really nice. So nice that you could spend your life there, even if beaches aren't really your thing. Even if someone points out that nothing, at first glance, distinguishes it from so many other beaches, and that as such there's no point in describing it, the moment you set foot on it, you know what happiness is: infinitely long, wide, with a gentle slope, bordered by leafy palm and banana trees if you want a bit of shade, extra-fine sand of a coral hue, water at 84 degrees: it is exceptional. This beach inspires such definitive peace, relaxation, and harmony that you don't feel like moving. Any sorrowful ideations instantly dissolve, past recollections and future prospects are banished. Facing the Flores Sea, you feel nothing but a sense of the perpetual present, perpetually pleasant.

Naturally, that sea does present some disadvantages. Its waters aren't terribly secure, for example, because of pirates, who since forever have abounded in the area, but in that regard things have changed somewhat. While the pirates still cultivate the same look—bandanna in their hair, earring, machine gun slung across bare chest, eyes dilated by phenyl-ethylamine, and grimacing with all their chipped teeth—their techniques have nonetheless evolved—updated weaponry, long-distance motion detectors, ultrarapid speedboats, GPS —as have their targets. And while their MO is still radical, they no longer prey, as in the olden days, on humble fishing boats: their sphere of action now extends to anything that moves on water, from solitary navigators to cargo ships, ocean liners, and giant container vessels. That said, the Flores Sea having become less trafficked, the pirates are generally busy elsewhere, most often to the northeast, in the Philippine Sea, where the mercantile flow is denser and better provisioned.

Annoyance-wise, these waves also, of course, harbor some disreputable species in their bosom. You can find various bothersome types, such as the moray eel or the sea serpent, though these are rarely encountered, spending most of their time hiding in their crevices. And anyway, you don't get anything for nothing, these annoyances are negligible, and the beach at Bira is surely the gentlest, most welcoming, most secure spot in the world, you can't see any reason to be elsewhere. You stretch out, you doze off, you turn over after reapplying your layer of cream at maximum SPF as the sun beats down until the sudden tropical nightfall, from one instant to the next like a stage curtain, but we're not there yet: for the moment, Louise Tourneur and Cedric Ballester, each on her or his beach towel, expose themselves to the ultraviolet, dance with sunburn, bullfight with carcinomas: good lord, how nice this all is.

It's five thirty when Dorothée Lopez joins them, large canvas bag on her shoulder, rolled raffia mat under one arm, radio/cassette player dangling from the other arm. Though Lopez has changed for the beach, her outfit is not particularly balneal: wearing white leather short-shorts and a vest, anchored by calf-length boots and topped by a cowboy hat, she's sporting extremely large sunglasses shaped like the wings of a fluorescent bat. Lopez trumpets a superfluous hello, Cedric and Louise open one eye each and grunt a monosyllable.

Dorothée Lopez unrolls her mat, sits down on it with an exhalation, asks how the water is, while looking for a station on her boom box. You can't get anything on this piece of junk, she grouses before finally coming to a Thai rock station blaring "Om Pra Mah Pood" by Sek Loso and Bird Thongchai, which she turns up full blast, making the two youngsters jump, stand, and flee toward the waves. As Louise retraces her steps to grab a mask and snorkel, Dorothée orders: Hang on a minute, let me see your finger.

Dorothée Lopez examines the index finger where the cut is already smaller: all that remains, coagulated in the hollow of the interphalangeal joint, is a minuscule beadlet of blood, no more obtrusive than a pinhead, and it's nothing serious, Lopez diagnoses, you're good to go—nothing like seawater to heal a wound. Louise heads off, catches up to, then passes Ballester, who, feet in the coastal interface, is still hesitating to plunge, letting the waves, with their long, frothy tongues, lick his toes and massage his instep.

Louise puts on her flippers, adjusts the strap of her mask, fits the snorkel into her mouth, then dives in: vibrant silence, scarcely disturbed by the echo of the bubbles, refracted sunlight on a valley of sand, and soon the fish appear, alone or in schools, in all colors and shapes, crested or bearded, bearers of antennae or draggers of veils, ornamented with festoons or braids, decorated with stripes of all stripes, polymorphous stars, squares, dots. As much as the jungle was disappointing, so is the sea plentiful, and Louise Tourneur is finally alone and at peace, protected, calm, and far from everything, but then a monster appears.

This is a thirty-seven-year-old monster, seventeen feet and nine inches long, weighing a ton and a half, presenting in the form of a large oblong mass, muscular and sinewy, bodywork in light gray and white. Constantly hungering for flesh, whether animal or human, living or dead, the monster is capable of locating the latter at more than a thousand yards' distance, thanks to the sensory receptors bristling on its skull: it reacts straightaway, and its sharply profiled fuselage, its hydrodynamic shroud, its shell of scales with aligned points allow for rapid progress, with instant acceleration.

This new character was hanging around the area, going about its business, when an internal alarm signal mobilized it, triggering a precise search, and it went on the hunt. Its fixed eyelids never blink, its cold, empty, obstinate, psychopathic eyes possess an acuity far superior to a human's, and its hearing and sense of smell can unhesitatingly detect the tiniest drop of blood in five million liters of water.

It's thus that, armed with outsize dentition, infinitely renewed by a conveyor belt effect, the monster is rushing toward Louise Tourneur. It is now ten yards away from her and very soon five yards, then less than one: its jaws open wide on twin sixfold rows of four hundred triangular, flat, barbed, crenellated incisors, then shut.

32

ON THURSDAY, I received the photo.

Every Thursday I went downstairs to check the mailboxes. Not so much my own, which I seldom opened, but that was the day when many of the weekly magazines arrived, and as I think I mentioned, I sometimes extracted the ones that stuck out messily from the neighboring slots, in a personal bid for maintaining harmony in the lobby. That day, I withdrew a *Paris Match* and an *Express* before verifying the possible contents of my box, just in case: among the flyers for a pizzeria that had already closed, a gym that had just opened, and an all-purpose repair service was a sealed envelope with no return address that might have been sitting there for several days. I nearly tossed it out unopened, since real estate agencies sometimes pull that trick to lure you in, but instead I stuck it between the magazines, forgot about it until midafternoon, then remembered. It contained only a press photo, probably cut from a newspaper, judging from the quality, of Chairman Franck Terrail.

So that was who I was supposed to take care of. I had sort of imagined it, among other possibilities, but without really believing it: despite what I had more or less understood about the multiple personalities of Jean-François Bardot, he didn't seem capable of so radical a plan. Regardless, it would be a daunting task. Having first made a name for himself within a small left-leaning Gaullist movement, Terrail had then drifted into other ephemeral formations, blowing with the wind, before founding the IPF. Though he had never gotten more than 2 or 2.2 percent of the vote, through perseverance he had nonetheless ended up acquiring a certain political visibility. Over time, he had even become a personality. A minor personality, but a personality.

In any event, the disappearance of this personality, whose name and political prestige resounded more strongly with public opinion than his wife's, would not fail to cause a stir, even more so if the nature of that disappearance was, as Bardot had mandated, violent. Its public impact would bear no comparison to Nicole Tourneur's recent misadventure, the fiasco of which was plain to see. Given this, I had a weighty responsibility, and I gauged what I'd gotten myself into. I could have refused the deal, of course, having no guarantees; but since it had been take-it-or-leave-it, and since I'd had every reason to take it and had taken it, I now had to go do it. I decided to proceed methodically, insofar as I was able, for the work was new to me. And I had to worry about my own person before studying that of Franck Terrail.

My person would need to take its sweet time to prepare the action. Not wanting anyone to hurry or harass me, I deemed it wise to cut myself off from the few people I knew, and especially from my silent partner, whom I didn't wish to run into during the process. It seemed fitting to burn my fragile social footbridges and perhaps take lodgings elsewhere. I thought it best to avoid rue Erlanger for a while. Now I just had to decide where to go.

Since staying in a hotel was not within my habits or my means, I briefly considered the ruins of the shopping center: though the reconstruction work was at a standstill, several modules had already been set up on its outskirts, intended to house the workers. As those sheds were unoccupied, I could have squatted in one: highly economical, close to home, therefore no expatriation, and no one would have thought to look for me there. However, this would have required logistics; moreover, the climate was ill suited for habitation, as those facilities were no doubt unheated at the moment.

I reasoned with myself. I could, after all, use the money Bardot had allocated, and I'd still have plenty left over if all went well. Besides, it would help my surveillance if I stayed physically close to Terrail, so as to familiarize myself with his schedule, habits, entourage, and protection. Determining the ideal time and place to carry out my mission presupposed a well-planned study. Breaking with my economic habits, I ended up taking a hotel room on rue de Javel, ten minutes on foot from Quai de Grenelle, not too far from his place, and, especially, not too expensive.

The modest rates of the Hotel Welcome were justified by the state of the room: a small table, a chair, a cold-water sink facing a bed with sticky sheets and a mattress covered in old hairs; by the shared bathroom facilities on the landing: cursory toilet, scalding or freezing shower with no middle ground; by the steep, narrow, dark stairway; and by the nonexistent soundproofing, which granted me intimate knowledge of my floormates, mainly young, impecunious foreign tourists. No elevator or television or bar, coffee maker out of service: the establishment had more in common with a youth hostel than with a hotel stricto sensu, but anyway, I was in the zone.

From there, I began observing the comings and goings of Chairman Terrail. Every morning I posted myself behind an advertising billboard at the foot of his tower and waited.

Terrail came out nearly every day, accompanied by his dry, swarthy, Latin-looking aide-de-camp, whom I'd already noticed in the building near Boucicaut waiting for the elevator with his boss. When they merely took a stroll around the neighborhood to get some air, I tailed them on foot as best I could, but I had to let them go when they headed off for parts unknown in the aide's little yellow Honda.

When you're on foot, trailing someone has its limits, and what I didn't foresee spoke volumes about my inexperience. Reluctantly, as I hated dilapidating my capital, I rented a car of a status commensurate with that of the hotel. I hadn't driven a car in a long time and had some trouble getting used to it, but it came back fairly quickly. Besides, they might have stripped me of my civic rights after the Paris–Zurich incident, but they had let me keep my driver's license. So now I could follow Terrail wherever he went.

It soon became apparent that he mainly went to medical appointments, which wasn't illogical at his age, when the GP is no longer enough, when one must subject oneself increasingly to specialists. There comes a time when everything erodes a bit more with each passing day, not to mention the wear and tear due to power: from the digestive realm to the urogenital empire, from the cardiac principality to the pulmonary duchy, under the increasingly fragile protection of the fortified *limes* of the epidermis and the control, year in and year out, of the cerebral episcopate, these potentates ultimately run short of breath. They then have to ping-pong from test to exam, analysis to sample, lab to pharmacy, constantly trailing behind some expert or other in anticipation of the geriatrician and, sooner or later, the coroner and his certificate. And indeed, my job was to call that coroner to Franck Terrail's side a bit earlier than planned.

That's when it hit me: people are vulnerable at the doctor's. Susceptible to the physician's omnipotence, for one, and even more so to the outside world. As a moment of extreme subjugation in which one finds oneself defenseless and unprotected, the medical consult seemed the ideal occasion to intervene—once the practitioner was neutralized, which shouldn't be too hard. All I had to do was identify the right moment, when the patient's total dependence would make him easier to get to, when his influenceability was at its acme: chest scan or lumbar puncture, dental extraction or rectal probe, I'd have my pick.

33

FRANCK Terrail—whom we find still supine in his unkempt bathrobe on the couch in his study, no longer able even to fall back on the Augustan anthology stuffed with photographs that procured him so much pleasure—is not in good shape and we can understand why: alone, distraught, at twenty to noon, the weather snowy without snowing, and the radio playing Mahler's Symphony No. 3.

Well, let's not exaggerate, Franck isn't as alone as all that: young Flax showed up that morning to bring him his mail, representatives from the Belfort section—Belfort has always been loyal to him—said they'd come by in the late afternoon, and, in the kitchen, Luigi Pannone is making him garlic risotto for lunch. That said, he'll be even more distraught once he learns about the drama that occurred in Sulawesi. But we're not there yet, for as these lines are being written, Louise Tourneur's tragic accident has not yet been announced under our skies. We'll get on it.

Franck, then, is in the doldrums. We had nonetheless seen him full of pep during the Caen rally, but maybe that was his swan song, his last speech as leader, and why not his last adult action. At present, he'd be incapable of such valor; he's able only to snivel over and over about Louise's flight to distant climes even after he opened the doors of power to her. As to Nicole's reappearance, all the signs are that he's indifferent. He naturally had to look relieved for form's sake, but in reality that return was highly inconvenient, upsetting as it did his succession plan—anyway, it's been quite a while since the Terrail-Tourneur couple was intimate, for at least three years each has occupied a separate apartment. Without bringing himself to admit it to anyone, not even Pannone, he would not have been displeased had Nicole disappeared for good; moreover, he's called her only once since her return, at the beginning of her stay at the Percy hospital.

In the distance, in the kitchen, we hear the ringtone of Pannone's mobile—an electro rendition of the "Hunters' Chorus" from *Der Freischütz*—followed by a brief, indistinct confabulation, and here's Luigi at the door of the study, looking uncertain, wiping his hands on his apron. That was Dorothée, he announces. She's coming up. Shall I add a plate? Terrail just has time to fix his bathrobe, run a comb through his hair, the doorbell rings, Dorothée Lopez appears.

She looks to be in a state. Her outfit is less elaborate than usual: chestnut-colored suit and flat shoes, minimal makeup. Eyelids puffy, on the verge of tears. She barely says hello. Drops into a chair, her bag rolling around on her knees. Pulls from that bag a pack of Kleenex, blows her nose. Shuts her eyes, takes a long breath, then launches into the story of the fatal accident. We'll let her tell it, we know it already. And there you have it, she concludes with a sob, a shark. A fucking piece-of-shit shark, she sniffles, pardon my grief.

Franck Terrail stands up after a pause, walks to the window, and stands motionless, his massive back silhouetted against a background of white sky. Silence. Dorothée Lopez is folded into her chair, face buried in her hands. You could have let us know immediately from over there, Pannone gently points out, as soon as it happened. You got no idea,

Luigi, mumbles Lopez from the hollows of her palms, last thing on our minds. Emergency services in those countries are a joke. And dealing with Cedric, he's a wreck, she exhales. And then all the steps you have to go through, the police, hospitals, local authorities. I'll spare you the part about gathering up the remains, repatriating the body, or what's left of it, she again dissolves in tears.

I understand, murmurs Pannone. And Ballester? he pretends to worry. In shock, Lopez summarizes. Straight to the convalescent home. I'm starting up my treatment again too. Pannone nods, another silence before the "Hunters' Chorus" sounds in the distance once more: Pannone rushes to the kitchen, picks up his phone, sees Francis Delahouère's number, rolls his eyes. I was calling to see if there was any news, Delahouère says innocently, while gesturing to the others to be quiet. Before answering, Pannone lowers the flame on his risotto, then outlines the situation.

Ah, I'm devastated, Delahouère declares with another sign for the others to shut up, I'm so sorry to hear it, Luigi, really so sorry, it's a great loss. Tell Franck, well, you know what to tell him. He hangs up and turns toward the others: Chanelle, Bardot, Bloch-Besnard flanked by Labroche, once more gathered in the apartment near Boucicaut, who give him questioning looks. It's the girl, Delahouère announces, little Louise. Dead. An accident. Jesus Christ, Bardot exhales. This changes everything, Chanelle summarizes. She wouldn't be pulling the same trick as her mother, would she? ventures Labroche. Shut your face, Brandon, grumbles Bloch-Besnard.

Everything has in fact been turned topsy-turvy. First Nicole, whom they thought themselves rid of, came back— even if, after the failure of her media coup, she now seems out of the running—and now Louise is gone, just as her promotion threatened to get in everyone's way, first and foremost that of Mozzigonacci's crew. Time to analyze this new data and draw the appropriate conclusions.

Which are unambiguous. This isn't the time to get rid of Franck, Chanelle deems and Bloch-Besnard seconds. Not that they should rally behind him, but they no longer have any reason to do away with him. He might still be useful, judges Delahouère, until we can find someone better. We might even need him more than ever, he analyzes, regency situations can have certain advantages. So we have to cancel the operation, Chanelle decrees, find this Fulmard as fast as possible and deactivate him. Moreover and besides, to be safe, we should increase Franck's protection, Luigi isn't enough. Do you know anyone who could watch over him 24-7?

I could, Labroche boldly offers. Oh, shut up already, Brandon, Bloch-Besnard grumbles again. Jacky, come on, Chanelle protests, stop ragging on the kid all the time, he's one of our best assets. Okay, Labroche, that works, you'll be in charge of that. Don't let Franck out of your sight, starting this afternoon. Pannone might not take it too well, objects an offended Bloch-Besnard. I know how to talk to Luigi, Delahouère claims, I'll explain it to him. Right, says Chanelle, anything else?

What a world, Bardot muses. First we wanted to eliminate Franck and now we want just the opposite. That's politics, Jean-François, Chanelle nervously sidesteps, that's how it works. Your job now is to neutralize your guy. Remember, Fulmard is only an amateur, Bardot moderates, he's not very skilled. Amateurs can be the most dangerous, Chanelle reminds them, we all know something about that. You're able to get to him, right? I'll do my best, Bardot acquiesces.

34

HAVING chosen my MO (though still lacking a few details), studied it from every angle, and judged it sound, I no longer felt it necessary to continue my surveillance. Not seeing why I should freeze my nuts off in a car or behind a billboard, I returned the rental to the agency and went back to the cozy warmth of the hotel, even if, in the afternoon, given the diminished residency, the management often shut off the radiators.

All in all, I was getting used to that hotel. I felt less cut off from the world than in the apartment on rue Erlanger. Living there full-time, I had the leisure to listen all day long to the noisy comings and goings and the booming, multilingual, often sozzled exclamations, proclamations, and interpellations of the low-budget tourists. Then at night I could hear the cries and moans of their coituses, weakened or stimulated by beer, easier to understand than their utterances, the sounds of copulation needing no translation: they're more or less the same everywhere, everyone knows perfectly well what they mean, a kind of Esperanto that hadn't fizzled.

Such an environment wasn't unpleasant. What most people call nuisances on the contrary gave me a certain comfort. For me, the voices and traffic in the hallways indicated a refreshing energy. As for the nocturnal clamors that at other times I would have considered disturbances of my pleasure, they in fact helped me sleep.

In the mornings, if I didn't feel like staying in my room, or on afternoons when the heating was suspended for too long, I went for a walk up and down the street. Though three times longer than mine, it inspired no more enthusiasm. Moreover, while the buildings on rue Erlanger could lay claim to a certain stylistic unity, rue de Javel, rather disparate in that regard, consisted of an unlovely sampling of the architectural fashions that had succeeded each other since it was first paved.

From the humble common plaster to the boastful facade in mirrored glass, from the sociable cheap brick of the interwar years to the enameled red-and-ocher brick under serrated rooftops, from the penniless post-Haussmannish to the destitute Louis-Philippoid, from Empire to equally tired art deco, rue de Javel was but a succession of heteroclite buildings in unscrupulously mismatched materials. Featuring abstruse windowless facades with faded tiles, or others in the raw concrete of an outmoded avant-garde, or with smoked plexiglass balconies or dusty faux-bow windows, these constructions were mostly unsigned by their authors, left there like anonymous letters.

It was while loitering around the end of that street, checking out the area near the Oudin-Barthélemy imaging clinic, where I planned to make my move, that I saw Chairman Terrail for the penultimate time: he was coming out, flanked not only by his Latin assistant but also by a burly young man half his age, his round face topped by a beige snap-brim hat. As it was threatening rain, I preferred not to linger, and went back to the Hotel Welcome.

I didn't go directly to my room, but hung out for a moment in the Welcome's entrance hall. Instead of a classic hotel lobby, this was a miserable room furnished with mismatched tables and chairs. Behind the empty bar, a shelf populated by dusty bottles held a television broadcasting some mounted trotting races in Paray-le-Monial, then in Cagnes-sur-Mer. I took a seat, gazing at the horses, musing over the lineaments of my plan.

It was then that these lineaments suddenly and harmoniously fell into place in my mind. I stood, walked back up rue de Javel under the newly falling rain to the Oudin-Barthélemy clinic, and went in. I'm not sure quite how I managed it, but, while getting around the receptionist by bombarding her with endless questions, I deciphered upside down in her appointment book the elements I needed: an acronym, a day, a time, a first name, and a last name: MRI, Friday, 3:15, Franck, Terrail. I couldn't have asked for better.

35

MAGNETIC resonance imaging, or MRI for short, has no equal if you want unhurried access to a subject undergoing a medical test, and if you wish to make of him what you will. Should you be nurturing such a plan, there's nothing more suitable than that technology.

Consider the evidence. Naked under a gown and strapped to an examination bed, wearing a noise-canceling helmet, the subject is enclosed in a tube that is open at both ends, in the heart of an imposing machine set up in a large, empty room. One might note that this machine consists of an enormous magnet whose traction pulls the body's hydrogen atoms in one direction, which allows one to observe said body in depth—one might note it, that is, if one is seeking to learn, but the question is academic: we're not here to observe or to learn, we're here to do harm.

Now, on the one hand, the narrowness of the tube prevents the subject from moving his limbs, and thus from being able to defend himself; and on the other, the openings at both ends allow you to intervene from the top or bottom, as you prefer. Moreover, there's no need to act silently, the patient being deafened by his helmet; better still, as the test lasts a good half hour, you have all the time in the world to operate. No doubt about it, if you have to act upon someone and, in my case, terminate him, the MRI is the ideal procedure, and I couldn't recommend it more highly.

Of course, you aren't entirely alone: a protective window separates the large room from a control booth in which a technician oversees the process and gathers data. If he wishes, that technician could occasionally glance through that window at the machine and its living contents, but generally speaking he's too busy with his control panel, too absorbed in his screens, on which he can see the whole inside of his patient's body, in color and three dimensions, for him to also look at the patient himself.

Early that Friday afternoon, I went through the door of the Oudin-Barthélemy clinic, walked unhesitatingly past the receptionist, and gave her a smile; I don't know if she recognized me, but she returned the smile before diving back into her appointment book, and I plunged into the guts of the clinic without anyone asking me a thing. From a random coat peg in an empty corridor, I snatched a white smock that I put on over my raincoat, which allowed me to feel I was passing unnoticed, then tried to find my way. Without too much difficulty, I came to a door marked MRI UNIT. Verifying that Bardot's pistol was firmly in my waistband, I glanced around and took a few deep breaths before pushing that door open.

Once inside, I caught my breath and courageously advanced toward the apparatus, looked it over: it inspired fear. The size of an SUV made of very thick metal, cream-colored and more or less cylindrical in form, it looked to weigh about fifteen tons and resembled the turbo reactor of a jumbo jet with a large fuselage, of the Ilyushin or McDonnell Douglas variety, with a round porthole bored into it at dead center, and from the opening at one end I saw emerge the two bare pink feet of Chairman Terrail.

There was my goal. But before getting to work, I glanced over at the control booth, and behind the glass I could see the technician, wearing a white smock like mine, bent over his consoles and video screens, which must have been showing him, in sections and on every spatial plane, the chairman's organs. He was a handsome, frail-seeming young man of inoffensive aspect, with the look of a pharmacy assistant; over his shoulder I made out Terrail's adjunct, who was also observing his boss's insides on the screen. Both of them seemed engrossed, without a glance at the machine room or, therefore, at me; I could get on with it.

Having placed myself as near as possible to the porthole, I was about to pull Bardot's weapon from my waistband and do what they had asked: aim inside the porthole, near the middle. But what I hadn't foreseen, what no one had warned me about, was that the machine then started up with an infernal commotion.

I don't know how else to describe the tumult produced by the MRI, so multiform and powerful that it was paralyzing, preventing me from moving forward and even from seeing where I was: a chaotic unfurling of enormous sounds, like an alarm siren, an 18-wheeler's horn, and a jackhammer all mixed together, alternating with mind-numbing jigsaw solos, monstrous duos for crusher and stamping press, vociferous trios for chain saw, grand organs, and rock drill on a counterpoint of a prehistoric ondes Martenot, the whole thing punctuated by constant and contradictory percussion, without order or relation, as if fourteen deaf, psychopathic drummers were facing off in a rage.

No use stopping up my ears, the monstrous concert invaded me not only through them but through the entire surface of my body. I was even at the point of turning tail, it was so unbearable. But at practically the same instant, even while deafened by the din, I nonetheless heard a noise very different from that of the machine, and at the same time felt a strong impact in my chest, not really localized but scattered throughout my person, as if a truck had just slammed into me. What I didn't have time to understand, what I would understand only later or maybe never, was that the magnetic force of the MRI had just yanked from my waistband the— unfortunately metal—weapon given to me by Bardot. I saw the pistol fly across the room and slam against a wall, and in its flight, no doubt, discharge one of its bullets in the direction of my plexus. I fell to the floor with eyes closed.

36

I OPENED them almost immediately. At first I thought I couldn't get up, but I managed, gradually, on all fours, then more or less upright. Taking advantage of the fact that the technician and Terrail's bodyguard were still absorbed in monitoring the chairman's entrails, I lurched unnoticed toward the door of the MRI unit.

Luckily, the corridor was still empty, and I quickly tried to gauge the extent of the damage to my anatomy. A small perforation was visible on my smock, to the lower left of the thorax, and under it my jacket was also perforated, and blood was beginning to spread on my shirt in the same spot. I got rid of the smock, pulled down the flaps of my jacket, and buttoned my raincoat before heading to the lobby, doing my best not to stumble. Absorbed in her appointment register, the receptionist neither saw nor smiled at me, sparing me additional effort, and when I left the Oudin-Barthélemy clinic at the top of rue de Javel, it was snowing.

Sometimes, provident taxi drivers park in front of hospitals or medical centers, standing ready for the people coming out: the latter often form a weakened, not overly choosy, and generally solvent population, the qualities necessary for a satisfactory clientele. This was fortunately the case: two or three cars were waiting near the clinic, their rooftop lights attesting to their availability. I climbed into the first in line, a tannish Škoda, and collapsed onto the back seat without letting too much show. I was starting to have trouble breathing, couldn't immediately indicate my destination—for a moment, furthermore, I wasn't sure what it was—and only when the driver asked without turning around where I was heading did I give, out of habit, the name rue Erlanger.

When he offered me a choice of route, as they sometimes do, I answered that the simplest was best, laboring to firm up my voice. It was in fact as simple as could be, as I knew: you only had to get to rue de la Convention, which was nearby, go down it and across the Seine, after which you were practically there. He nodded, started up, I pressed back a bit farther into my seat, and we rode.

It was snowing, but just a little, really only a little, just the occasional flake, enough for the driver to turn on his wipers, not enough to keep them from squeaking on the windshield, and he himself kept silent. I briefly looked at his wide shoulders, his massive neck, his blank gaze in the rearview, then I turned toward the window and watched the building facades of rue de la Convention parading by. A laundry, a bank branch, a superette, a bar: up until then I was coexisting more or less peacefully with my wound; it was after passing the bar that things took a turn for the worse. I began to feel that my hemorrhage was increasing in volume, given the blood that began soaking through the fabrics of my jacket and raincoat and then, with increasing abundance, began to flow down my legs and drain perpendicularly onto the seat. I didn't panic too much, I stupidly pressed the wound with my hand, I would be home in a few minutes, I also stupidly told myself that it would pass.

There is a traffic light at the foot of rue de la Convention, at the corner of Quai André Citroën, before you continue onto Pont Mirabeau; my taxi stopped at this light. Taking advantage of the pause, my driver examined me in turn in his rearview mirror. I'm not sure what I looked like, but he asked in a not very sympathetic voice if I was feeling okay. As I didn't answer, he turned around and saw the scene: blood all over my clothes, on the seat, on my hands, no doubt some on my face, which was reduced to a clenched grimace. The driver let out a coarse exclamation, but, the light having changed to green, idiots began honking behind us and he was forced to start across the bridge.

Sometimes, too, well-meaning taxi drivers show themselves to be attentive to the condition of their charges. Confronted with situations like mine, they take the matter in hand, call in to their dispatcher, and rush you to the emergency room. This was not the case with mine, who flew into a rage, shouting that I had mucked up his seats and, braking abruptly in the middle of the bridge, drove the Škoda up onto the curb past the bike lane. Letting the car straddle half the sidewalk without cutting the engine, he brusquely got out, crossed over behind the car, and ran toward the door on my side, which he yanked open. He leaned over, lifted me by the armpits, and transported me none too gently onto the sidewalk, where he dropped me near the parapet. I heard him swear some more, saw his taxi speed off, and it was still snowing a little.

I remained perfectly conscious, even if the inert look of my body, tossed askew onto the ground, might make you think otherwise. I dragged myself to the parapet and rested my shoulders against it, my head leaning on the cast iron. Pont Mirabeau has a handsome parapet, of a gentle linden green and prettily sculpted; through an opening in the guard-rail I could easily make out the Seine below, looking soiled and immobile, like me. Weakness suddenly came over me but I continued to watch the river. I noticed a yacht heading up it slowly, two seagulls had landed on the roof of its cabin, and then a woman emerged from that cabin and opened a promotional umbrella, I tried to read what it said but it was too far away, I gave up, closed my eyes, felt a snowflake land on one of my eyelids, then it must have melted, a drop of water slid down my temple.

OTHER NEW YORK REVIEW CLASSICS

For a complete list of titles, visit www.nyrb.com.

DANTE ALIGHIERI Purgatorio; translated by D. M. Black
JEAN AMÉRY Charles Bovary, Country Doctor: Portrait of a Simple Man
KINGSLEY AMIS Take a Girl Like You
IVO ANDRIĆ Omer Pasha Latas
CLAUDE ANET Ariane, A Russian Girl
HANNAH ARENDT Rahel Varnhagen: The Life of a Jewish Woman
OĞUZ ATAY Waiting for the Fear
DIANA ATHILL Don't Look at Me Like That
DIANA ATHILL Instead of a Letter
WILLIAM ATTAWAY Blood on the Forge
DOROTHY BAKER Cassandra at the Wedding
S. JOSEPHINE BAKER Fighting for Life
HONORÉ DE BALZAC The Lily in the Valley
HONORÉ DE BALZAC The Unknown Masterpiece *and* Gambara
POLINA BARSKOVA Living Pictures
VICKI BAUM Grand Hotel
SYBILLE BEDFORD A Favorite of the Gods *and* A Compass Error
ROSALIND BELBEN The Limit
STEPHEN BENATAR Wish Her Safe at Home
FRANS G. BENGTSSON The Long Ships
GEORGES BERNANOS Mouchette
ADOLFO BIOY CASARES The Invention of Morel
CAROLINE BLACKWOOD Great Granny Webster
HENRI BOSCO The Child and the River
EMMANUEL BOVE My Friends
MALCOLM BRALY On the Yard
MILLEN BRAND The Outward Room
JOHN HORNE BURNS The Gallery
ROBERT BURTON The Anatomy of Melancholy
DINO BUZZATI The Bewitched Bourgeois: Fifty Stories
DINO BUZZATI A Love Affair
DINO BUZZATI The Singularity
DINO BUZZATI The Stronghold
INÈS CAGNATI Free Day
LEONORA CARRINGTON The Hearing Trumpet
CAMILO JOSÉ CELA The Hive
BLAISE CENDRARS Moravagine
EILEEN CHANG Written on Water
FRANÇOIS-RENÉ DE CHATEAUBRIAND Memoirs from Beyond the Grave, 1800–1815
AMIT CHAUDHURI Afternoon Raag
AMIT CHAUDHURI Freedom Song
AMIT CHAUDHURI A Strange and Sublime Address
ANTON CHEKHOV The Prank: The Best of Young Chekhov
JEAN-PAUL CLÉBERT Paris Vagabond
LUCILLE CLIFTON Generations: A Memoir
RICHARD COBB Paris and Elsewhere
RACHEL COHEN A Chance Meeting: American Encounters
COLETTE Chéri *and* The End of Chéri
D.G. COMPTON The Continuous Katherine Mortenhoe
IVY COMPTON-BURNETT A House and Its Head
BARBARA COMYNS The Juniper Tree